Twin
Troubles

*Here are some other
Redfeather Books you will enjoy*

---

*The Curse of the Trouble Dolls
by Dian Curtis Regan

Lavender
by Karen Hesse

Sable
by Karen Hesse

*Snakes Are Nothing to Sneeze At
by Gabrielle Charbonnet

*Stargone John
by Ellen Kindt McKenzie

Tutu Much Ballet
by Gabrielle Charbonnet

*Twin Surprises
by Susan Beth Pfeffer

*Available in paperback

Twin Troubles

Susan Beth Pfeffer

Illustrated by
Abby Carter

A Redfeather Book

Henry Holt and Company   *New York*

Published by Henry Holt and Company, Inc.,
115 West 18th Street, New York, New York 10011.
Published simultaneously in Canada by Fitzhenry & Whiteside Ltd.,
195 Allstate Parkway, Markham, Ontario L3R 4T8.

Library of Congress Cataloging-in-Publication Data
Pfeffer, Susan Beth.
    Twin troubles / Susan Beth Pfeffer; illustrated by Abby Carter.
    (A Redfeather book)
    Summary: Eight-year-old Crista has the worst week of her
life, experiencing bad times at school and at home, but when
her twin sister, Betsy, tries to sympathize by sharing her bad
times, it causes a fight.
    [1. Twins—Fiction. 2. Sisters—Fiction. 3. Family life—
Fiction.] I. Carter, Abby, ill. II. Title. III. Series:
Redfeather books.
PZ7.P44855Tx 1992
[Fic]—dc20   92-5773

ISBN 0-8050-2146-9 (hardcover)
10 9 8 7 6 5 4 3 2 1
ISBN 0-8050-3272-X (paperback)
10 9 8 7 6 5 4 3 2 1

First published in hardcover in 1992 by Henry Holt and Company, Inc.
First Redfeather paperback edition, 1994

Printed in the United States of America on acid-free paper. ∞

*To the wonderful people at
the Miracle Mile Bagel Bakery
of Middletown, New York*

Contents

School Troubles

"Crista, what is five times six?"

Crista Linz had been staring out the window, thinking about her kitten Misty. She and her twin sister, Betsy, had brought their kittens home just the day before. Crista worried that Misty would get lost in her new home, or that Marty, Crista and Betsy's baby brother, might fall on Misty and squoosh her. For every two steps Marty took, he fell once.

"Crista, I asked you what is five times six?"

Crista heard her name and realized the other kids were looking at her. She thought she heard a couple of giggles. "I'm sorry," she said.

"Are you sorry because you weren't listening or

because you don't know the answer?" her teacher, Mr. Lopez, asked.

"I don't know," Crista said. "I mean both. Either. I mean either."

This time everybody laughed except Crista. Even Mr. Lopez had a smile on his face.

"Are you paying attention now?" he asked.

Crista nodded. She was listening with every part of her ears.

"What is five times six?" Mr. Lopez asked.

"That's easy," Crista said, relieved that the question was one she could answer. "Six times six is thirty-six."

Everyone laughed even harder then, except for Mr. Lopez. Crista looked around for her sister Betsy. Betsy wasn't laughing. She was just shaking her head and mouthing something to Crista.

Crista could usually understand what Betsy was saying even if she couldn't hear her. Their mother sometimes said the twins didn't need words, they knew each other so well. But this time Crista had no idea what Betsy was trying to tell her.

"Look at me, Crista," Mr. Lopez said. "I know you know the answer."

"I just told you the answer," Crista said. "Six times six is thirty-six."

The class really laughed then. Crista hadn't heard them laugh so hard since the clown had been at the school assembly. And that was way back in first grade.

"Betsy, I saw you trying to help Crista out," Mr. Lopez said. "Do you want to tell the whole class the answer, or just your sister?"

"Five times six is thirty," Betsy said. "But Crista was right. Six times six *is* thirty-six."

"Both answers are right," Mr. Lopez said. "Thank you, Betsy."

Betsy smiled at Crista. Crista tried to smile back.

"Crista, what lesson have you learned just now?" Mr. Lopez asked.

Crista wasn't sure. "I should pay more attention to what Betsy's telling me?" she asked.

"Not when she's trying to give you the answers," Mr. Lopez said. "Instead, pay more attention to your lessons. Daydreaming is fine. We all need to do it sometimes, but not during arithmetic."

Betsy raised her hand. "Sometimes I don't pay attention," she said. "Sometimes I daydream just like Crista."

"Betsy and Crista do everything the same," Jane said. Jane was a good friend of both the twins.

"We feel the same too," Betsy said. "When Crista's sad, I'm sad. And she knows what I know, so she knew what six times five was too. Honest, Mr. Lopez."

Mr. Lopez looked at the twins and laughed. "I'm sure she did," he said. "Crista, what's six times four?"

Crista's face turned bright red. "I'm sorry," she said. "I was thinking about how Betsy and I are alike."

"I was too," Betsy said. "Crista and I were having the exact same thought."

"I told you they were the same," Jane said.

"Amazing," Mr. Lopez said. "Class, let's all tell Crista what six times four is."

"Twenty-four," the class all said, except for a couple of kids who said "Twenty-six."

"Very good," Mr. Lopez said. "Are we ready to move on?"

Crista certainly was. Actually, by then, she was ready to move out.

Supper Troubles

"**D**id anything interesting happen in school today?" Crista's father asked that night at supper. The family was sitting around the dining-room table. They always ate together—Mr. and Mrs. Linz, and Crista and Betsy and Marty and their big sister, Grace. Grace was twelve, and sometimes really interesting things happened to her just because she was big.

"I had a science test," Grace said. "I think I did okay on it. And Jennifer Daley puked in the middle of gym class."

"No puking talk at the dinner table," Mrs. Linz said. She always said that when someone wanted to talk about puking.

Marty banged his spoon against the high chair.

Sometimes even if he hadn't puked, his tray looked like he had.

"Did anything else happen in school, Grace?" Mr. Linz asked. "Did you get your spelling test back?"

"I got a ninety," Grace said. "Hardly anyone got a hundred. It's hard to when Mrs. Smith gives a spelling test. She doesn't say the words loud enough. She mumbles, you know. We all try to hear her, but we can't."

"Have any of you told her that?" Mr. Linz asked.

Grace nodded. "We did right after the first spelling test," she said. "And Mrs. Smith said it was good for us. That way we'd really have to listen."

"Ah ah ah ah ah ah ah," Marty said. No one listened to him.

"Chips wants something to eat," Betsy said. Her kitten was named Chips. He was black with a white face. Misty was gray with a white face. Chips was trying to climb up Betsy's leg. "Can I give him something, Mom?"

"Not from your plate," Mrs. Linz said. "If you

do, he'll get into the habit of asking all the time. So will Misty. Cats get fed cat food and people get fed people food. I think you should tell Chips that rule right now."

Betsy helped Chips up her leg. He sat on her lap and purred. "No food," Betsy said. "But I'll pet you."

Chips purred even louder.

"Where's Misty?" Grace asked.

"I don't know," Crista said. She'd played with Misty when they'd gotten home from school, but she hadn't seen her since. Maybe Marty had squooshed her. "Mommy, have you seen Misty?"

"I see her," Betsy said. "She's in the corner there. I think she's hiding from us."

"Why should she hide?" Crista asked.

"Maybe she's seen the way Marty eats," Grace said.

"Misty's more of a watching kind of cat," Mrs. Linz said. "Chips is more of a climbing kind of cat. Just because they're brother and sister doesn't mean they have the same kind of personality."

"Crista and I do," Betsy said. "We're just the same all the time."

"You're twins," Mr. Linz said. "Twins are different from kittens. Besides, you and Crista aren't exactly alike either. Just more alike than most other people."

"We are too exactly alike," Betsy said. "Today in school, when Crista wasn't listening, I wasn't listening either."

"What are you talking about?" Mrs. Linz asked.

Crista wished Betsy hadn't brought it up. "Mr. Lopez asked me a question and I got it wrong," she said. "So he told all of us we shouldn't daydream."

"But the thing was, I was daydreaming too," Betsy said. "Just not as hard as Crista was. So I knew the answer when Mr. Lopez called on me. But I almost wouldn't have."

"How could you almost not know an answer?" Grace asked.

"I almost said thirty-five," Betsy said. "And that would have been even worse than what Crista did. She said thirty-six, when the answer was thirty."

"Why would thirty-five have been worse?" Grace asked. "It's closer to thirty than thirty-six is."

"But we were doing our six tables," Betsy said. "If I'd said thirty-five, then Mr. Lopez would have known I thought we were doing our five tables. I was really thinking about Chips."

"And I was thinking about Misty," Crista said. "We really are exactly alike."

"If you're going to be exactly alike, could you be exactly alike and listen to your teacher?" Mrs. Linz asked. "Instead of being exactly alike about your kittens?"

Crista and Betsy nodded. Marty threw his spoon at Misty, who ran out of the dining room to safety.

"You won't see her again tonight," Grace said.

"That's okay, Crista," Betsy said. "You can play with Chips and me. Right, Chips?"

Chips purred. Crista tried to smile, but she wished she could play with her own kitten instead. Maybe she and Betsy should give Misty and Chips lessons in being more alike.

Store Troubles

"I'm going to the bookstore, Mom," Grace said after school the next day. "Okay?"

"Don't stay too long," Mrs. Linz said. "And don't spend too much."

"I won't," Grace said.

"Can I go with you?" Crista asked.

Grace looked down at her sister. "You won't do anything dumb?" she asked.

"I won't," Crista said. "I promise."

"All right," Grace said.

Crista ran into her room. Betsy was on her bed, playing with Chips and Misty. Misty seemed to be having a great time. "I'm going to the bookstore with Grace," Crista said. "Want to come?"

Betsy shook her head. "I'll stay here with the kittens," she said.

Crista nodded. She opened the little box where she kept money she was saving, and she took out two dollar bills and three quarters and two dimes. That was what the new Jenny Archer book cost in paperback.

"Hurry up!" Grace called. Crista ran out of the room and joined Grace at the door.

"I'm going to buy the new Jenny Archer," Crista told Grace. "She's my favorite."

"Okay," Grace said. "You have enough money?"

Crista nodded happily. She loved reading. She'd already read the book she was going to buy at school, but now she could own her own copy. She'd been saving her money for three weeks to buy the book. She could hardly wait until she got it home.

Betsy liked to read, but not as much as Crista did. That was one way the twins were a little different from each other. Crista wondered if Misty liked to read more than Chips. She giggled.

"No giggling at the bookstore," Grace said. "If

you just stand there giggling, everyone will think you're crazy."

"I'm sorry," Crista said, even though she wasn't. She'd learned a long time ago it made things easier just to say you were sorry to Grace. Grace didn't care if you meant it.

The bookstore was four blocks away. Crista loved living only four blocks from a bookstore. She couldn't wait until she was old enough to walk there by herself. She would have skipped to get there faster, but she didn't think Grace would like that. She didn't feel like saying "I'm sorry" twice in one block, either. So she just walked.

"Don't do anything dumb," Grace said again as they entered the store. "I don't want the world to know what a dumb kid sister I have."

"I won't, I promise," Crista said. Someday she'd probably tell Marty not to do anything dumb. Right now just about everything he did was dumb, but he was a baby, so it looked cute. Crista tried to picture Marty eight years old. All she could see was a baby her own size, wearing an enormous diaper. She giggled loudly.

"No giggling," Grace whispered angrily. "I warned you."

"Sorry," Crista said. It was hard not to giggle at a giant Marty. She coughed instead.

Grace went to the section of the bookstore she was interested in, and Crista walked over to the younger kids' books. There it was, the new Jenny Archer. It looked even better in paperback than it had in hardback. She could hardly wait to own it.

She looked at all the other books for sale. They looked good too, but she knew what she was going to buy. She'd known for three weeks. She carried the book to the counter to pay for it.

"Are you paying for this yourself?" the sales clerk asked.

Crista nodded.

"And you have enough money?" the sales clerk asked.

Crista felt the money in her pocket. She nodded again.

The sales clerk rang up the cost on the cash

register. "That's three dollars and thirteen cents," she said.

"No it isn't," Crista said. "It's two dollars and ninety-five cents." She pointed to the cost of the book. It was right there on the cover. Two dollars and ninety-five cents.

"There's eighteen cents' sales tax," the sales clerk said. "Three dollars and thirteen cents, please."

"I don't have three dollars and thirteen cents," Crista said. "I only have two dollars and ninety-five cents. Do I have to pay sales tax? I'm only eight."

The clerk laughed. "That's really cute, kid," she said. "But eight or eighty, we all have to pay."

Crista looked over at Grace. She didn't dare ask her for the money. Instead she took the book and put it back where she found it. Next week she'd have three dollars and thirteen cents. But it just wasn't fair that she couldn't buy the book she wanted right then and there. And she hated it when she made a mistake and people said it was cute.

Betsy's Troubles

"Did you buy anything?" Betsy asked when Crista got home from the store.

Crista shook her head. "I didn't have enough money," she said. "I forgot about sales tax. They laughed at me."

"That's terrible," Betsy said.

Crista felt like crying. She hated being laughed at, and now it had happened twice in two days.

Chips and Misty didn't seem to care about Crista's troubles. They kept chasing each other on Betsy's bed. Sometimes they ran right over Betsy to get to each other. Betsy giggled every time they did that. Crista wished Betsy would stop.

"Did Grace see what happened?" Betsy asked.

"No," Crista said.

· 19

"Well, that's good," Betsy said. "The same thing happened to me once. I was with Grace at the store, and I wanted to buy a little teddy bear. It was so cute. Not as cute as Chips, but cute, and I thought I had enough money, so I took it to the counter and said I wanted to buy it. And the clerk asked me to show her all my money, and I did, and I was fifty-five cents short. And the clerk asked me if I knew how to count, and did I know what money was, and it was terrible."

"What did you do?" Crista asked. She wondered what would happen if she picked Misty up and brought her to her bed to play. Betsy picked Chips up all the time, and Chips loved it.

"I asked Grace for the money," Betsy said. "Oh look, Crista."

Crista looked. Misty was trying to catch her own tail, and Chips was running around her. They were going faster and faster. Betsy was laughing really hard, and soon even Crista was laughing. Kittens didn't mind if you laughed at them.

Misty stopped very fast, and Chips fell on top of her. In an instant they were both snoring.

"Maybe we should sleep that way," Betsy said.

"I think it's easier if you have fur," Crista said. "Did Grace give you the money?" She didn't want to tell Betsy she'd been too scared to ask Grace herself.

"No," Betsy said. "She got real mad at me. She said she was never taking me to a store again. She said little kids shouldn't be let into stores, that they should just wait outside while older kids shopped. She said she was sorry she ever had twin sisters and she never ever wanted to see me again. You know. She said Grace stuff."

"Did you say you were sorry?" Crista asked.

"I did not," Betsy said. "I said she was mean and rotten and I stuck my tongue out at her. Like this." Betsy stuck her tongue out at Crista. She looked pretty silly.

"You look like Chips getting ready to give Misty a bath," Crista said.

"I do?" Betsy asked. She hopped off the bed to check herself out in the mirror. "I need more fur," she said, once she'd looked.

"What did Grace do?" Crista asked. She would

never have the nerve to stick her tongue out at Grace in a store.

"She screamed for Mom," Betsy said, getting back on her bed. The kittens kept sleeping. "Mom was with you and Marty. Marty was real little then. Mom told Grace not to scream and me not to bother Grace."

"Did you mind?" Crista asked.

"I minded a lot," Betsy said. "It was terrible. Grace was mad at me and Mom was mad at me and I didn't even get the teddy bear I wanted. It was almost the worst thing that ever happened to me. It was a lot worse than what happened to you today."

"Why?" Crista asked. She figured what had happened to her had been pretty bad.

"Grace didn't get mad at you and Mom didn't get mad at you," Betsy said. "And we only live four blocks from the bookstore. You can go back next week and buy the book. When I went back to buy the teddy bear, it was months later, and they didn't have it anymore. See what I mean."

"I do," Crista said, but she felt like she did when she apologized to Grace and didn't mean it. What happened to Betsy was definitely bad, but Crista didn't see why it was worse than what had happened to her. Nobody had laughed at Betsy. It didn't seem fair that no matter how bad things that happened to Betsy were, things that happened to Crista were just a little bit worse.

·5·

Once-in-a-Lifetime Troubles

C rista sat in her bedroom and looked down at her homework. It was just arithmetic. Usually she had no trouble with her arithmetic homework. But today she couldn't seem to remember any of the answers.

She could hear Betsy and Jane in the living room. They were playing with the kittens. Crista wanted to be there with them, but her mother had told her to finish her homework first.

Six times seven was . . . Crista knew she knew. She knew all her multiplication tables better even than Betsy. So why had Betsy raced through her homework while Crista wasn't even halfway through yet?

Six times seven. Crista certainly knew what six

times five was. Thirty, thirty, thirty. She still remembered how everyone had laughed at her.

Mr. Lopez had said if you couldn't remember how much six times seven was, see if you remembered how much seven times six was, since the answer was the same. Crista looked at her homework and tried to picture seven times six, but nothing came out.

"Chips is the cutest kitten ever!" Jane cried.

"I think he's cuter than Misty," Betsy said. "But don't tell Crista that."

Crista sighed. Lots of times when Betsy didn't want her to know something, she forgot to whisper and Crista found out anyway.

"Misty's cute too," Jane said. "But you're right. Chips is cuter."

Chips was cuter than Misty, Crista thought. But Misty was prettier. And when they were all grown up, it was going to be better for Misty that she was pretty and not cute. When they grew up, Misty was going to be the prettiest cat in the world.

"Oh, look at them!" Jane shouted. "I can't believe they're doing that."

What? Crista wondered. The kittens always seemed to do their cutest stuff when she wasn't around.

"I wish I had a kitten," Jane said. "If I had a kitten, I'd want it to be just like Chips."

That was too much. Nobody was paying attention to poor Misty. The homework would just have to wait.

Crista left her bedroom and went into the living room to see what the kittens were doing. They were curled up next to each other, sleeping.

"They're sleeping?" she asked. "Is that what you were screaming about?"

"We were not screaming," Jane said.

"You should have seen them a minute ago," Betsy said. "Chips was standing up, right on his back legs. He looked so cute. And Misty was running around, and she didn't look where she was going and she ran right into him and knocked him over. It was really funny."

"I bet it was," Crista said. She wished she'd seen it. "Do you think they'll do it again?"

"Maybe," Betsy said.

"No," Jane said. "It was what my mother calls a once-in-a-lifetime experience. She says kittens and babies only do the really best stuff once, and if you don't see it then, you never see it."

"Marty does the same stuff over and over," Crista said.

"Not the same cute stuff," Jane said. "That he only does once. You probably never get to see his cute stuff because you're in school."

"That's right," Betsy said. "I bet we've missed lots of cute stuff."

"And not just Marty's," Jane said. "The kittens', too. I bet they do lots and lots of cute stuff when you're not around."

"They do plenty of cute stuff when we're here," Crista said. "I've seem them do cute stuff."

"I wonder what I've missed," Betsy said. "I bet I've missed practically every cute thing they've ever done."

"Why do you say that?" Crista asked.

"I'm outside more than you are," Betsy said. "Lots of times you'll be sitting around reading and

I'll be outside playing. I bet the kittens do tons of cute stuff when you're reading, and all you have to do is look up and see them. I can't see them from outside."

Jane shook her head. "You've probably missed every cute thing they ever did," she said to Betsy. "Crista's so lucky, getting to see them all the time."

"Crista's the luckiest one," Betsy said. "She's much luckier than I am."

Crista looked at both of them and at the sleeping kittens. If she was so lucky, why did she feel so bad?

Homework Troubles

"Come on, girls," Mr. Linz said that night after supper. "Let me see your homework."

"Here's mine," Grace said.

"Have you been working on your spelling words?" Mr. Linz asked.

Grace nodded. "I'm going to get a hundred next quiz," she said. "I know it."

"Good," her father said. "Betsy, Crista, show me your homework."

"I'm getting it!" Betsy called from their bedroom.

Crista sat at her chair. She'd forgotten all about finishing her homework. She and Betsy and Jane had tried for over an hour to get Chips and Misty to repeat their once-in-a-lifetime experience, but no matter how hard they'd tried, the kittens wouldn't do it. They'd done plenty of other cute things, but Chips didn't stand up and let Misty run into him. And every time the kittens didn't do it, Jane and Betsy would giggle, remembering how cute they'd been.

"Crista, where's your homework?" her father asked.

"I didn't finish it," she said.

"Why not?" her father asked. He didn't sound mad, but Crista knew he was. They were all supposed to do their homework before supper. That was the rule.

"I meant to, but I forgot," Crista said. "I'll finish it now."

"Were you having trouble with it?" her father asked. "Do you want me to help you?"

Crista shook her head. "I just forgot about finishing it," she said. "It won't take long. I'm sorry."

"Let me see it when you're done," her father said.

Crista went into her bedroom. Betsy was just about to walk out with her homework.

"I forgot about finishing," Crista said. "I heard you and Jane talking about the kittens, and I forgot my homework."

"That's terrible," Betsy said. "Can I help?"

"No," Crista said. "I can do it."

She sat alone in the bedroom and tried to remember six times seven. Pretty soon the answer came back to her, and she was able to do all her work.

She showed her father her homework. He didn't scold her, the way she was afraid he would. "Just remember, school is the most important thing," he said. "And doing your homework helps you do better in school."

Crista and Betsy went to bed early that night. The kittens were already asleep, curled up at the foot of Betsy's bed. They'd had a long day too, Crista thought, doing cute things when she wasn't looking.

"Did Daddy get mad at you?" Betsy asked.

"No," Crista said. "He just told me how important homework is."

"That's good," Betsy said. "He got mad at me and I was afraid he'd get mad at you, too."

"Why did he get mad at you?" Crista asked.

"He said it was my fault you hadn't finished," Betsy said. "Because I invited Jane over to play with the kittens. He said it was fine for me to play outside if you weren't through with your homework, but I shouldn't play inside, because then you could hear me and you wouldn't get your work done."

"What did Mommy say?" Crista asked.

"She said we both had to remember that no matter how much we loved the kittens, our schoolwork came first," Betsy said. "I tried to tell them about what Chips and Misty had done, and how we tried to get them to do it again just for you, but they said kittens were going to do cute stuff all the time and we had plenty of chances to see it and I'd better learn to be quiet when you were working. They said you were quiet when I was trying to work and I should do the same for you."

"It's hard to be noisy when you're reading," Crista said.

"I wish you'd remembered to finish your homework," Betsy said. "That way they wouldn't have scolded me."

"I'm sorry," Crista said. She'd lost track of how often she'd said she was sorry that week, but she knew it wasn't a once-in-a-lifetime experience.

Tooth Troubles

7

"Ouch!" Crista said the next morning.

"What's the matter?" her mother asked.

"My tooth hurts," Crista said.

"Is it bad?" her mother asked.

Crista nodded. "It started hurting during the night," she said. "And now it's even worse."

Her mother sighed. "Let me call the dentist," she said, "and see when he can see you. You go get dressed."

Crista did. When she came out, her mother had finished on the phone.

"We're seeing him right after school," her mother said.

"But there's a Brownie meeting then," Crista said.

· 37

"Sorry," her mother said. "Toothaches come first."

Crista's tooth hurt all during school that day. Her mother sent a note with her so the teachers didn't call on her. That was the only good thing that happened.

After school Crista's mother came to pick her up. Marty was strapped in his car seat in back. Much to Crista's surprise, Betsy joined them.

"Why aren't you going to the Brownie meeting?" Crista asked.

"I have a toothache too," Betsy said. "Ooh, it hurts."

Crista knew that whenever she caught a cold, Betsy got it also. Maybe toothaches were catching too.

"I'll see Crista first," Dr. Thaler said. Crista went into the room and climbed up on the dentist chair. Dr. Thaler asked her which tooth hurt, and Crista showed him. Dr. Thaler poked at the tooth with his instrument, and Crista cried out in pain.

"You have a cavity all right," Dr. Thaler said.

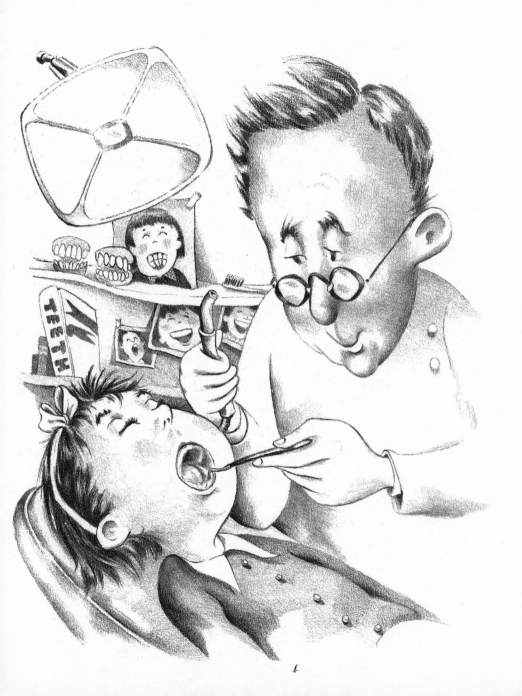

"I'm going to give you a shot of novocaine, Crista. The needle is going to hurt a little bit, but then your tooth will go numb, and you won't feel me drilling. Your mouth will just feel funny for a little while afterward, but there won't be any pain. All right?"

"All right," Crista said. She closed her eyes when Dr. Thaler gave her the shot. It hurt a little more than a little bit, but then there wasn't any pain, and before she knew it, he was all done.

"Betsy's turn," he said.

Crista waited with her mother and Marty. She waited for Marty to do something cute that she wouldn't ordinarily have a chance to see, but Marty only sat in his mother's lap and looked around. Crista wasn't surprised. Nothing was really cute at a dentist's office.

Betsy didn't take nearly as long as Crista. "Twin toothaches," Dr. Thaler said as he brought her out. "There was nothing the matter with Betsy's tooth."

"Then why did it hurt?" Crista asked.

"Because Betsy loves you, I guess," Dr. Thaler

said. "When you don't feel well, she doesn't feel well."

Mrs. Linz paid the dentist and drove them all home. "Crista's homework can wait tonight until after supper," she said. "Let's give the novocaine a chance to wear off. Betsy, why don't you get to work right now."

"All right," Betsy said.

Crista sat in the living room, waiting for the kittens to do something cute. But they were no more in the mood than Marty had been.

Misty was asleep on the sofa. Crista walked over to the sofa and sat down next to Misty. She petted the kitten. Misty purred, but she kept right on sleeping.

Crista picked Misty up. Maybe if she gave her a hug, Misty would wake up and do something cute. Misty purred and snored and never opened her eyes.

"Wake up, stupid," Crista said. She held Misty in her hands and gave her a shake. "Wake up and do something cute for me."

Misty woke up. Her eyes got real big and she

tried to jump out of Crista's grasp. Crista held onto her. Misty wiggled and squirmed, but Crista only held on tighter.

Then Misty scratched Crista's hand and pulled free. "Ouch!" Crista shouted.

Crista's mother came out of the kitchen. "Crista, what's the matter?" she asked.

"Misty scratched me," Crista said. "I was holding on to her and she scratched me."

"You don't need a Band-Aid," her mother said. "But be more careful next time. You can't hold a kitten too hard. They'll fight to get away."

Crista stared at her scratched hand. Her mouth throbbed. Her head hurt. She'd never felt worse in her life.

"Mommy!" she cried, and as soon as her mother was by her side, Crista began to sob.

Digging Up Troubles

"**W**hat's the matter, honey?" her mother asked. "Is it your hand?"

Crista shook her hand. "It's my life," she sobbed. "Everything is awful."

"Oh dear," her mother said. "Tell me about it."

"I wasn't paying attention in arithmetic and I didn't have enough money for my book and the kittens only do cute stuff when I'm not around and I didn't remember to do my homework and I had a toothache and Misty hates me."

"Oh dear, oh dear," her mother said. "It certainly sounds like you've had a terrible week."

"The worst," Crista said.

Crista's mother gave her a kiss. "We all have weeks like that sometimes," she said. "The important thing is to make the bad things stop."

Crista sniffled. "What can I do?" she asked.

"Let me think," her mother said. "Misty will love you again all on her own, you know. And your tooth will stop hurting once the novocaine wears off. And you'll be able to buy the book you want next week."

"Do I have to wait that long?" Crista asked. "I'd like things to get better right away."

"I have an idea," her mother said. "Why don't you go outside and dig a hole?"

"What?" Crista said.

"A hole," her mother said. "I remember my mother once told me to dig a hole and bury all my troubles in it. And you know, I felt a lot better once I did. Get your pail and shovel and dig a nice big hole and throw all the bad things that happened to you this week in it. Then you can throw the dirt over it, and all your troubles will go away."

Crista looked out the window. It was a pretty fall afternoon. The flowers were still blooming and the trees had red and orange leaves. "I'll need to dig a real big hole," she said.

"You can do it," her mother said. "I'll be in the kitchen with Marty and we'll both watch you dig."

Crista wasn't sure it was going to work, but her mother came up with lots of good ideas. She went to her bedroom and looked for her pail and shovel.

"What are you doing?" Betsy asked as Crista dug through their toy chest.

"I need my pail and shovel," Crista said.

"Why?" Betsy asked.

"Mommy told me to dig a hole," Crista said. She found what she was looking for and smiled. "I'll be outside digging," she said. "Bye."

"Bye," Betsy said.

Crista showed her mother the pail and shovel as she walked through the kitchen.

"Dig a nice deep hole," her mother said.

"Ah ah," Marty said.

Crista grabbed her jacket and put it on. She walked around the backyard, looking for the perfect place to dig a hole. Finally she decided on a spot just a few feet away from the kitchen window. That way her mother and Marty could see how well she was doing.

It had rained a few days before, and the ground was still soft. Crista enjoyed digging and making a pile of dirt next to the hole. She didn't use the pail, but she liked having it there by her just in case.

"That's a great hole," Betsy said.

Crista turned around and saw Betsy standing behind her, carrying her own pail and shovel.

"What are you doing?" she asked.

"Mommy said I should dig a hole too," Betsy said. "She said my week was pretty awful too and I'd feel better if I buried my troubles just like you."

"Oh," Crista said.

"I think I'll dig my hole right next to yours," Betsy said. "That way our troubles can keep each other company."

"Okay," Crista said. She started digging again.

Betsy began digging, and she worked very fast. In no time she'd caught up with Crista, and soon her hole was even bigger than her twin's.

"What are you doing?" Crista asked. "You don't need such a big hole."

"Of course I do," Betsy said. "I had a terrible week. Just like you."

"You did not!" Crista said. "I'm the one who had a terrible week."

"I had a worse week," Betsy said.

"Did not!"

"Did too!"

"Did not!" Crista shouted. She started throwing dirt back into her hole, and into Betsy's too, not caring where the dirt landed.

Twin Troubles

"Stop it!" Betsy said to Crista. "You're burying my troubles too."

"You don't have any troubles," Crista said. "I'm the one who got in trouble at school. I'm the one who didn't do her homework. I'm the one who had the cavity."

"Oh," Betsy said. "I thought I had troubles too."

"You thought you had a toothache," Crista said. "And you didn't."

"But my tooth hurt," Betsy said.

"You didn't have a cavity," Crista said. "You didn't get a shot of novocaine. You didn't have everything go numb."

"No," Betsy said.

"Does your tooth hurt now?" Crista asked.

Betsy felt all her teeth with her tongue. "No," she said. "My tooth stopped hurting when yours did."

"Nothing bad happened to you this week," Crista said. "Everything bad that happened, happened to me."

"Really?" Betsy asked. "It felt like all the bad stuff happened to me too."

Crista shook her head. "Just me, not you," she said.

"Daddy scolded me," Betsy said, "when you didn't do your homework."

Crista thought about it. "Okay," she said. "That was a bad thing that happened to you. But I was the one who forgot about her homework. So it was worse for me. And you got to see the kittens do cute stuff and Misty loves you and not me and I don't care that you didn't get to buy your teddy bear months ago. I didn't get to buy my book this week. I had the worst week of my life this week, and it doesn't make me feel any better when you say your week was even worse."

"I thought it did," Betsy said. "That's why I kept telling you all the bad stuff that happened to me. So you'd feel better."

"It didn't work," Crista said. "It made me sad and then it made me mad, but it never made me feel better."

"Oh," Betsy said. "I want you to feel better. What makes you feel better?"

"Digging a nice big hole," Crista said.

"Could I help you with your hole?" Betsy asked. "Your hole could join mine and then it would be the biggest hole ever. Would that help?"

"You'd give your hole to me?" Crista asked.

"Sure," Betsy said. "I gave my troubles to you."

"Okay," Crista said. "But I want to do all the digging."

"All right," Betsy said. "Can I watch?"

Crista nodded. She picked up her shovel and dug right next to Betsy's hole. It took a minute or two, but then the two holes became one.

"This hole is mine," Crista said. "Just for my troubles."

"Crista's trouble hole," Betsy said. "For burying all your troubles."

Crista threw a shovel's worth of dirt into the hole. "This is for not paying attention in school," she said. "And this is for not having enough money for my book."

"That's a good one," Betsy said. "That was a really good trouble."

"And this is for the kittens doing all their cute stuff when I'm not watching," Crista said. "And this is for forgetting to do my homework." She threw in two more shovels of dirt.

Betsy sat there watching. Crista saw she looked kind of sad.

"I think you should throw some dirt in too," Crista said. "For Daddy scolding you."

"Thank you," Betsy said, and she gave Crista a big smile. "I was hoping you'd let me."

"This is for cavities," Crista said. "Now do one for toothaches."

"This is for toothaches," Betsy said.

"This is for fighting with Betsy," Crista said.

"I'd rather have a hundred toothaches than fight with you," Betsy said.

"I don't think you can have a hundred tooth-aches," Crista said. "We don't have that many teeth."

"Not even together?" Betsy asked.

Crista shook her head.

"I'd still rather have a lot of toothaches than fight with you," Betsy said.

"Me too," Crista said. "Come on, let's finish with the hole."

The twins filled the big hole with all the dirt they'd dug out. When they finished, they walked into the kitchen together.

"Look at Marty," Betsy said. "He's so cute."

He was, too. He was crawling on the floor trying to pet Chips.

"Meow." Crista looked down and saw Misty standing on her hind legs, trying to climb up Crista's pants. Crista bent down and picked Misty up very carefully. The kitten climbed up her arm, and snuggled on Crista's shoulder. She purred

loudly and licked Crista's cheek.

"She's kissing you," Betsy said. "That is the cutest thing I've ever seen."

"Me too," Crista said. "This is very once-in-a-lifetime."

"The most I've ever seen," Betsy said.

"The most for me, too," Crista said.

"Meow," Misty said, and the twins knew it was the most once-in-a-lifetime experience for her as well.

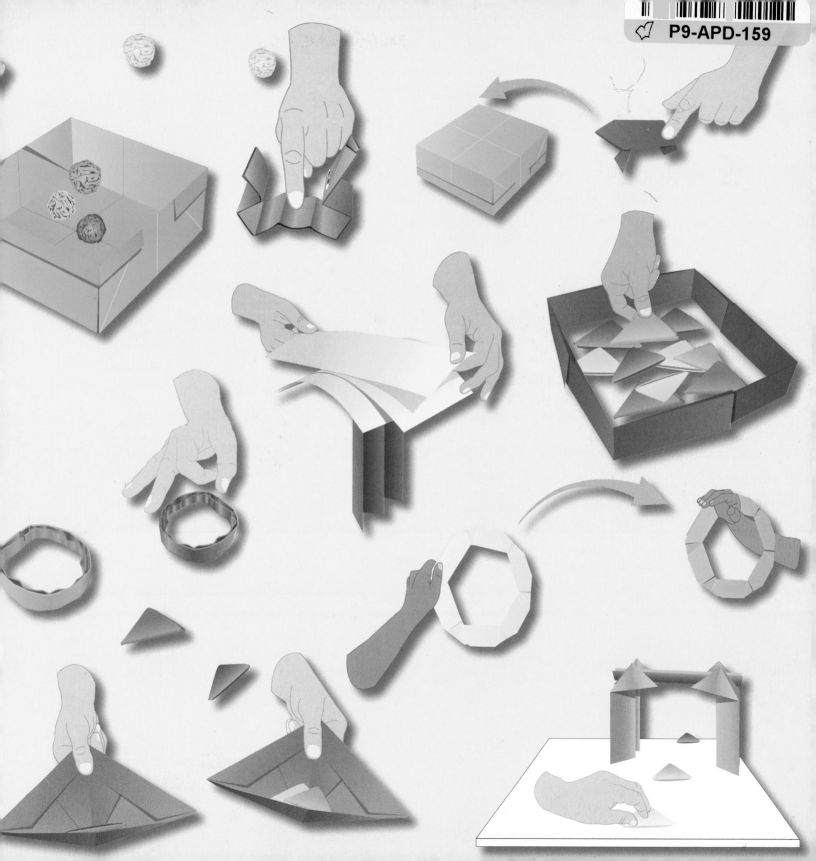

Published by Tuttle Publishing, an imprint of Periplus Editions (HK) Ltd., with editorial offices at
364 Innovation Drive, North Clarendon, Vermont 05759 U.S.A. and at 61 Tai Seng Avenue #02-12, Singapore 534167.

Copyright © 2010 Joel Stern
Graphic Designs by Konstantin Vints

Library of Congress Cataloging-in-Publication Data

Stern, Joel, 1953-
Origami games : hands-on fun for kids! / Joel Stern. -- 1st ed.
p. cm.
ISBN 978-4-8053-1068-7 (hardcover)
1. Origami. 2. Games. I. Title.
TT870.S7274 2010
736'.982--dc22
2009032928

ISBN 978-4-8053-1068-7

Distributed by
North America, Latin America & Europe
Tuttle Publishing, 364 Innovation Drive, North Clarendon, VT 05759-9436 U.S.A.
Tel: 1 (802) 773-8930; Fax: 1 (802) 773-6993
info@tuttlepublishing.com   www.tuttlepublishing.com

Japan
Tuttle Publishing, Yaekari Building, 3rd Floor, 5-4-12 Osaki, Shinagawa-ku, Tokyo 141 0032
Tel: (81) 3 5437-0171; Fax: (81) 3 5437-0755
tuttle-sales@gol.com

Asia Pacific
Berkeley Books Pte. Ltd., 61 Tai Seng Avenue #02-12, Singapore 534167
Tel: (65) 6280-1330; Fax: (65) 6280-6290
inquiries@periplus.com.sg   www.periplus.com

First edition
14 13 12 11 10   5 4 3 2 1
Printed in Singapore

Contents

Introduction

This book is different from most other origami books—it not only explains how to make origami, but also offers lots of ideas for games you can play with the finished origami models. And these origami pieces do not require a lot of experience; most are under ten steps.

PART I contains the diagrams for making the origami game pieces, which are presented in order of difficulty. The diagrams use the standard origami folding symbols recognized throughout the world (see the Symbols guide that follows). Most of the origami models in this book are my own creations; the rest are traditional, or variations of traditional designs. All are made from **standard U.S. letter-size (8 1/2 x 11-inch) paper**, which is easily available. With a few adjustments, they can also be folded from rectangles of other proportions, such as A4-size paper, available outside the United States.

PART II contains the games, which are suitable for ages two through adult. There are two kinds of games in this book—**competitive**, which allow players to test their skills against each other, using scorekeeping to determine a winner; and **collaborative**, which provide fun ways for players to work as a team. It's easy to change a competitive game into a collaborative one, and vice versa. The games appear in alphabetical order.

As you make the origami game pieces, you'll discover some of the surprising qualities of paper. How you fold it determines if it will stand stiffly to bear weight, spring over an obstacle, float through the air, or fall with a thud.

My Origami Games—in the back of the book—is an example of a form that lets you describe your own original games. When you get an idea for a game you can write it down, and share it with friends.

For teachers and parents, pages 89–91 discuss some of the educational and developmental benefits of origami, and offer ideas on how this book might be used in the classroom.

For more origami fun, take a look at page 92, which recommends additional resources such as origami books and paper, web sites, and online communities.

Let the games begin!

Symbols

The origami symbols used in this book are standard throughout the world. You'll find that as you become accustomed to working with them, you'll be able to read the diagrams without referring to the words.

Even though the letter size paper you'll use will be the same color on both sides, I use different shades of the same color in the diagrams to indicate the two sides of the paper.

Valley fold

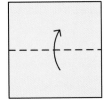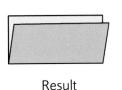

Result

This is a plain arrow. Because valley folds are so common in this book, I simply refer to them as "folds."

Mountain fold

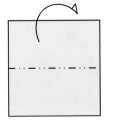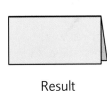

Result

This arrowhead is a right triangle.

Unfold

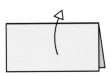

This arrowhead is an equilateral triangle.

Result.
Thin line shows an existing crease.

Fold and unfold

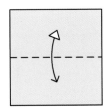

Result

The plain arrow shows the direction of the fold. The triangle shows the direction of the unfold.

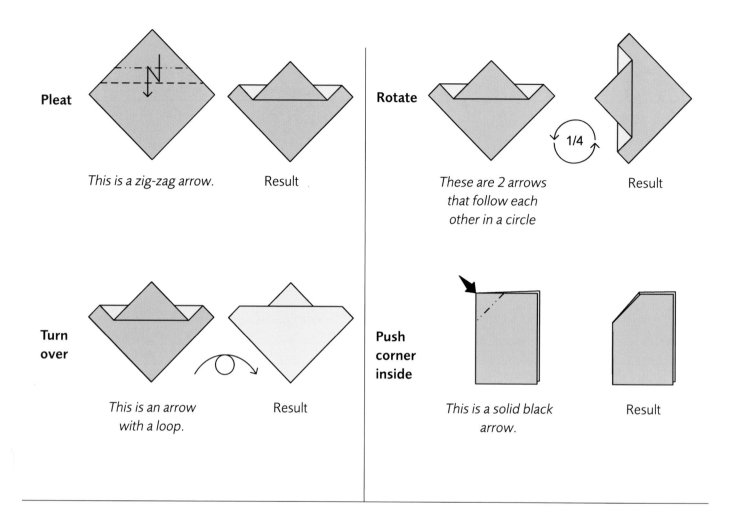

Pleat

This is a zig-zag arrow. Result

Rotate

These are 2 arrows that follow each other in a circle 1/4 Result

Turn over

This is an arrow with a loop. Result

Push corner inside

This is a solid black arrow. Result

Repeat steps on other flap

Beneath-the-surface view or guideline

Insert

Pinch

Part I

The Origami Game Pieces

Ghost

While doodling with a sheet of paper one day, I stopped at a certain point and asked myself what it reminded me of—a ghost! You can give it personality not only with the face you draw on it, but also by the way you position it.

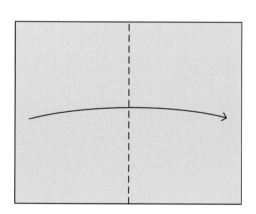

1 Fold the left edge to the right.

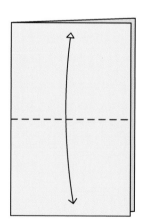

2 Fold and unfold the top edge to the bottom.

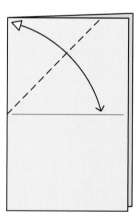

3 Fold and unfold the top left corner to the crease made in step 2.

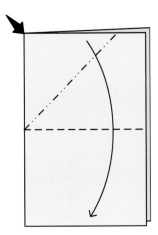

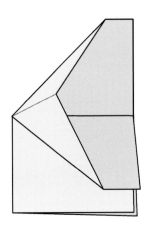

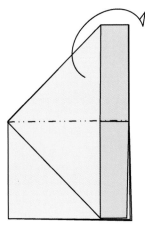

4 Bring the top edge of the near layer to the bottom, while squashing the point at the top left.

Step 4 in progress

5 Mountain-fold the top flap behind.

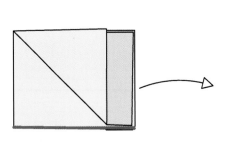

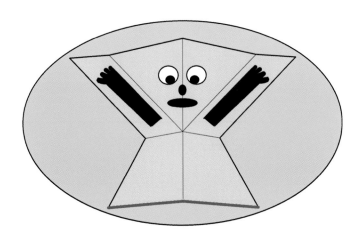

6 Open up the entire model, and stand it on a table along the edges indicated with red.

The Ghost.
Draw on a face and arms.

Glider

This is the traditional glider that I learned as a kid. It's certainly one of the easiest to make, and can stay on course for long distances.

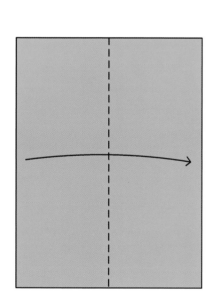

1 Fold the left edge to the right.

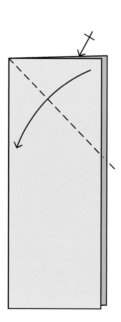

2 Fold the top edge of the front flap down to lie along the left edge. Repeat behind.

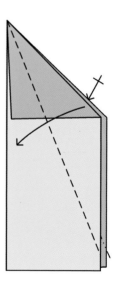

3 Fold the diagonal edge of the front flap to lie along the left edge. Repeat behind.

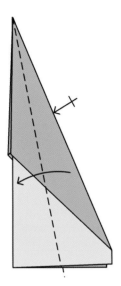 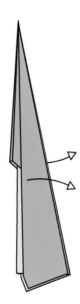 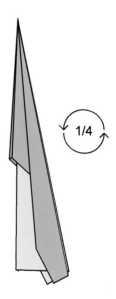

4 Fold the diagonal edge of the front flap to lie along the left edge. Repeat behind.

5 Open out the topmost layer slightly. Repeat behind.

6 Rotate the model 1/4 turn.

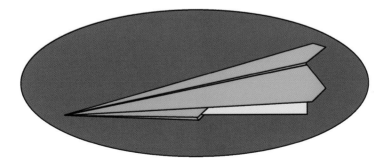

The Glider.

Game Board

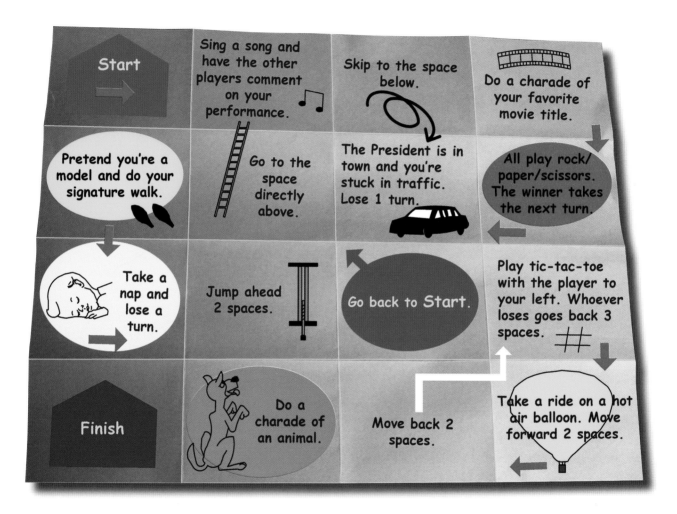

You could actually use any size rectangular paper to make a game board.
The fun is in coming up with the activities to do when you land on each spot.

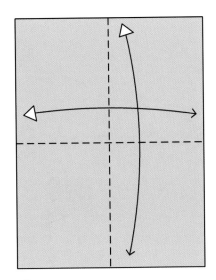 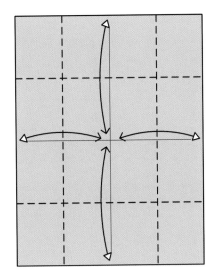 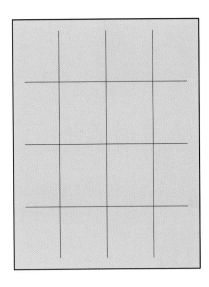

1 Fold and unfold the left edge to the right, and the top edge to the bottom.

2 Fold and unfold the four sides in to the creases you made in step 1.

The Game Board with 16 spaces.

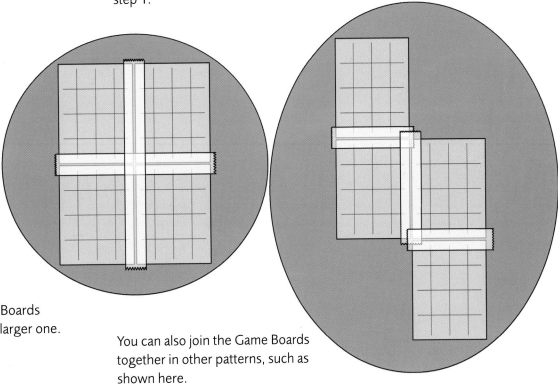

Tape several Game Boards together to make a larger one.

You can also join the Game Boards together in other patterns, such as shown here.

Zig-Zag Unit

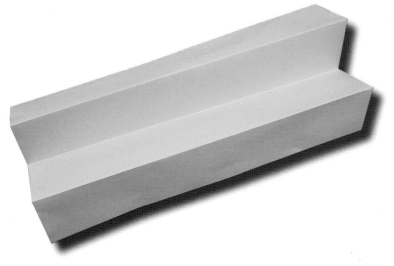

This simple fan-fold model has many different uses. It can bear weight, and can also connect to additional units to make different kinds of wall-like structures, like those used in the "Bull's-Eye" game (page 67).

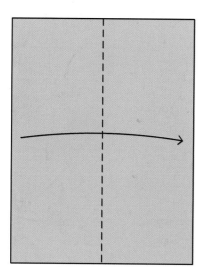

1 Fold the left edge to the right.

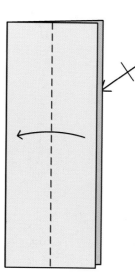

2 Fold the right edge back to the left. Repeat behind.

The Zig-Zag Unit.

Tube

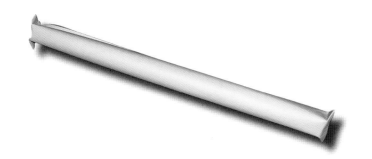

In this book the Tube is used in only one game—the "Ring Toss" (page 83), but it can also be used as a building block. You could make dozens of them and construct "Lincoln Log®"-type buildings.

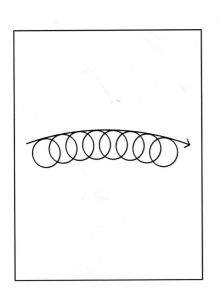

1 Roll the paper into a cylinder.

2 Press in the sides at the top, creating small triangular flaps in the front and back.

3 Fold the triangular flaps down in the front and back.

4 Repeat steps 2 and 3 on the other end.

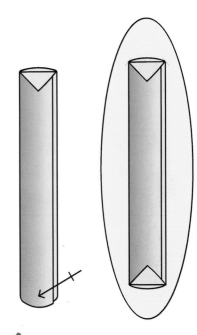

The Tube.

Sailboat

There are many origami sailboats, but this is one of a very few that you can blow on to send it sailing.

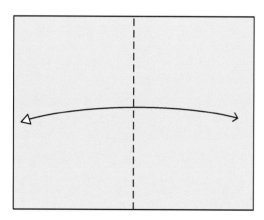

1 Fold and unfold the left edge to the right.

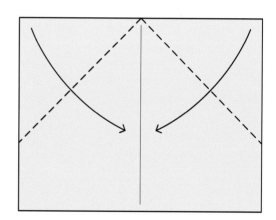

2 Fold the upper left and right corners to the center.

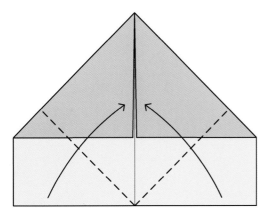

3 Fold the left and right portions of the bottom edge to the center.

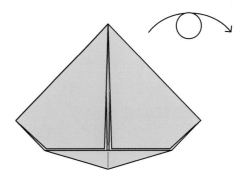

4 Fold the top of the model over the lower flaps.

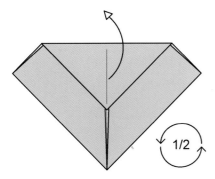

5 Lift up the flap you made in step 4 so that it stands out at 90 degrees. Then rotate the model 1/2 way around.

6 Turn the model over.

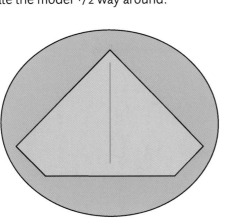

The Sailboat.

Wing

This wing doesn't fly, but because it has a large span, it's great for balancing. Besides using it with the Pyramid in the "Balancing Act" game (page 64), try balancing it on your finger and seeing how far you can walk before it falls off.

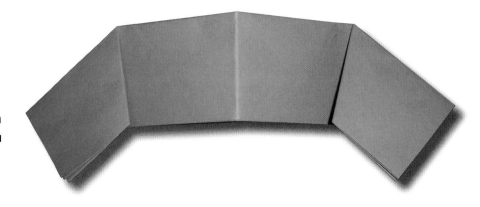

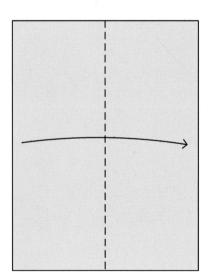

1 Fold the left edge to the right.

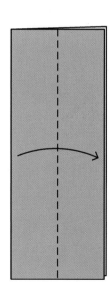

2 Fold the left edge to the right again.

3 Fold the bottom edge to the top.

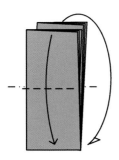

4 Fold the front and rear flaps to the bottom edge.

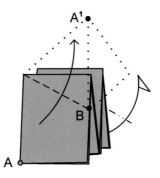

5 Fold corner A up and to the right to position A¹, so that it is positioned directly above point B. Repeat this behind.

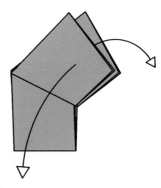

6 Open the wing by unfolding the front and rear flaps.

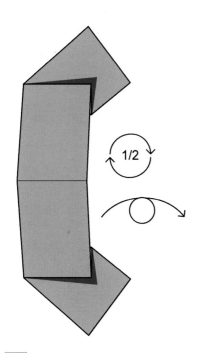

7 Turn the model over and rotate it ¹/₂ way around.

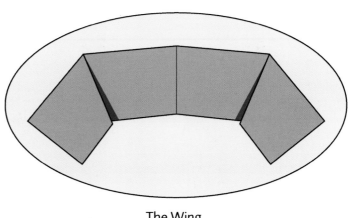

The Wing.

Dragon

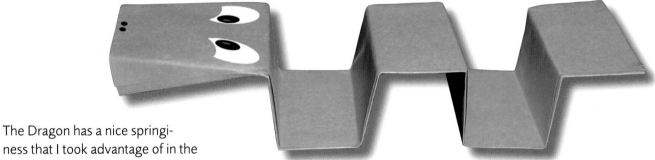

The Dragon has a nice springi-ness that I took advantage of in the games "Fill 'er Up" (page 70) and "Snap Dragon" (page 86). You'll have to use a little extra effort to fold the model in step 8, where it's particularly thick.

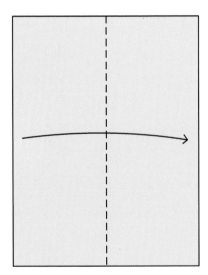

1 Fold the left edge to the right.

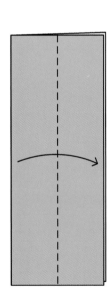

2 Fold the left edge to the right again.

3 Bring the right corner down so that it lies along the left edge, then make a pinch where the crease meets the right edge. Unfold.

4 Fold the top edge down along a line that meets the pinch you made in step 3 (down to the dotted guide line). Then unfold.

5 Fold the bottom edge to meet the crease you made in step 4.

6 Fold the top edge of the new flap down to the bottom.

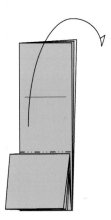

7 Mountain-fold the top portion of the model behind along a crease that coincides with the top of the small flap nearest the front.

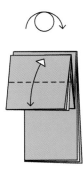

8 Fold and unfold the top edges (all thicknesses) to meet the bottom edge of the topmost flap. Turn the model over.

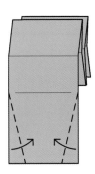

9 Fold the lower corners inward a little, beginning at the crease nearest the bottom edge. These will be the dragon's fangs.

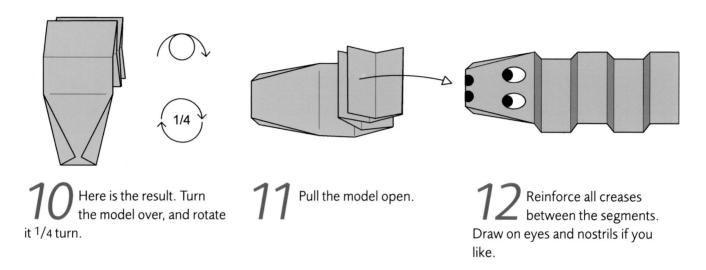

10 Here is the result. Turn the model over, and rotate it 1/4 turn.

11 Pull the model open.

12 Reinforce all creases between the segments. Draw on eyes and nostrils if you like.

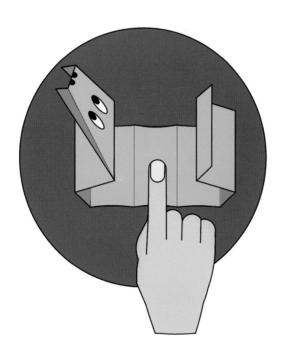

The Dragon. Pressing down in the middle of the body causes the front and back to snap up.

Box

My origami teacher Lillian Oppenheimer, who did more to spread origami through the West than anyone, always used to begin her origami classes with this model so that her students would have something in which to carry home their models. She often used magazine covers because they were stiffer than regular letter paper.

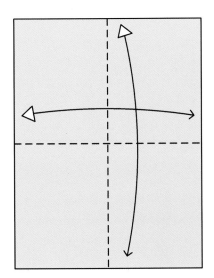

1 Fold and unfold the left edge to the right, and the top edge to the bottom.

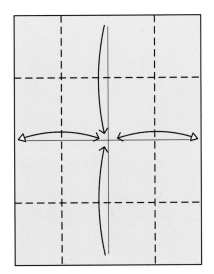

2 Fold and unfold the left and right edges to the center. Fold, but do not unfold, the top and bottom edges to the center.

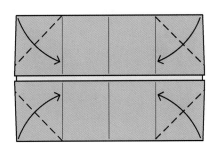

3 Fold the four corners to the creases.

Box | 23

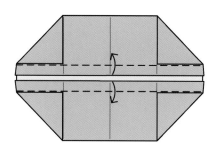 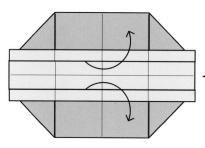 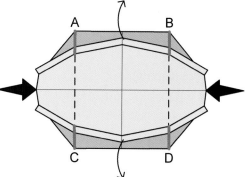

4 Fold the inside flaps outward from the center, covering up the triangular flaps you made in step 3.

5 Spread open the flat structure into three dimensions, pulling the top and bottom sections apart.

6 Continue spreading open the box, pushing in the sides, and pinching corners A, B, C and D (shown in red) to make the four walls stand upright.

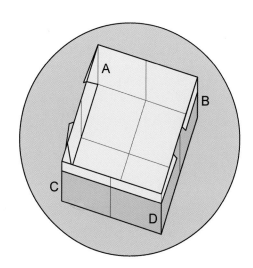

The Box. The four vertical corners A, B, C and D were made with pinches in step 6.

Basketball Hoop

No one knows who invented this origami model, but it's one of my favorites because it creates a complete game environment with just a few folds (plus a crumpled ball!)—see page 65.

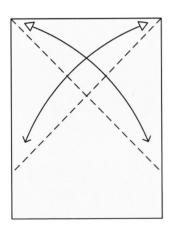

1 Fold and unfold the upper left and right corners to the opposite sides.

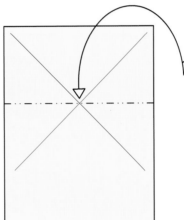

2 Mountain-fold and unfold the top edge down, so that the crease passes through the intersection of the creases made in step 1.

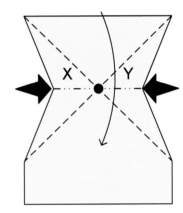

3 Press down the model at the dot, causing the shape to pop inside-out. Then, push in the sides while bringing down the top. Flaps X and Y will be created, and then hidden beneath the top flap.

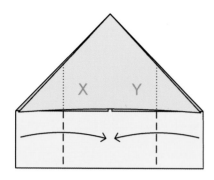 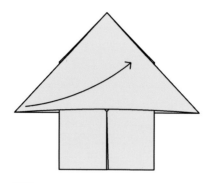 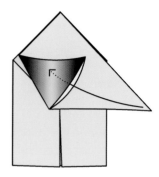

4 Note that flaps X and Y are now beneath the top flap. Valley-fold the left and right edges to meet in the center, beneath the triangular flap.

5 Swing the lower left corner up and to the right. *Do not crease*, and hold the flap in place as you do the next step.

6 Swing the lower right corner up and to the left, inserting it inside the flap on the left. The two flaps will stay in a rounded configuration.

7 Swing open the left and right flaps to enable the model to stand.

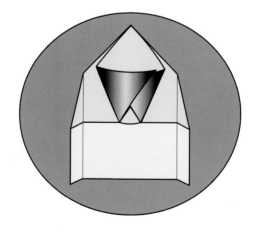

The Basketball Hoop.

Bowling Pin

This model was born from a doodle, when I overlapped one quarter flap over another. Once I saw that the structure could stand freely, I simply folded over the three corners to lock the shape.

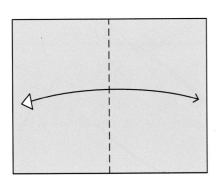

1 Fold and unfold the left edge to the right.

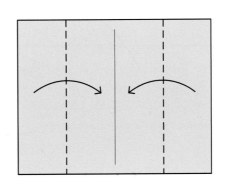

2 Fold the right and left edges to the center.

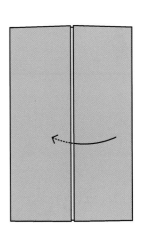

3 Feed the right flap behind the left flap, closing the model into a rigid 3-sided shape.

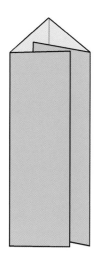

Step 3 in process.

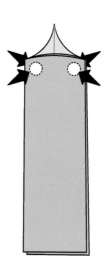

4 Pinch the left and right corners at the top at the dotted circles.

5 Proceeding clockwise, first valley-fold the right corner down at 45 degrees, which locks the open side of the model. Then mountain-fold the left corner behind. Finally, fold the rear corner forward.

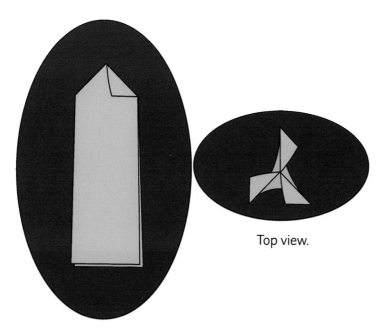

The Bowling Pin—front view.

Top view.

Catapult

I wanted a catapult that could project objects as far as possible. Having the flap at 45 degrees as shown in step 7 didn't provide enough of an arc, which is why I change the angle of the crease in step 8. You can bring the point further down for even greater projectile distance.

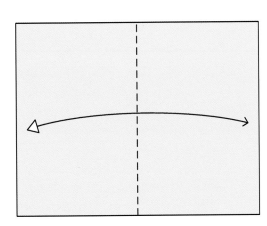

1 Fold and unfold the left edge to the right.

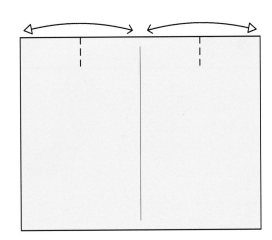

2 Bring the left and right edges to the center crease and make pinch marks.

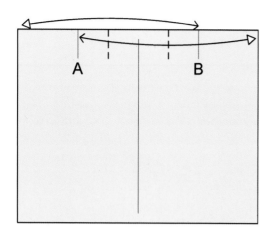

3 Bring the left edge to pinch mark B and make a new pinch. Bring the right edge to pinch mark A and make a new pinch.

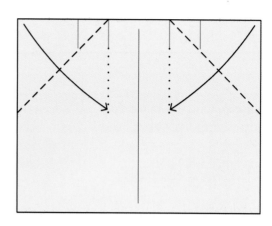

4 Fold the left and right top corners to align with extensions of the pinch marks you made in step 3.

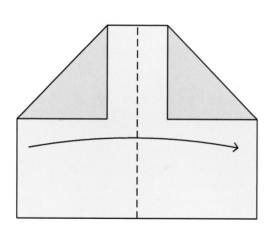

5 Fold the model in half.

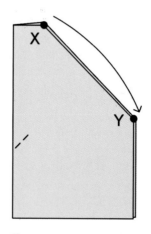

6 Bring corner X down to meet corner Y, and when they meet, make a small pinch at the left edge.

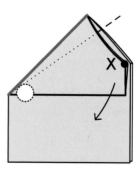

7 Holding the model loosely at the circle on the left, slide corner X down along the right edge of the model. The segment shown in red will be realigned. When the corner realigns with the right edge, crease the flap in that new position.

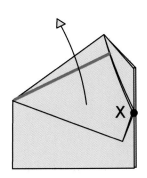

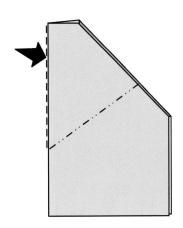

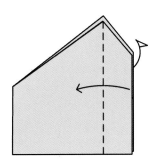

8 This drawing shows where corner X aligns with the right edge. Note the new position of the red segment. Now unfold to step 6.

9 Push the top portion of the left edge inside the model along the crease made in step 7, changing the mountain crease into a valley.

10 The top flap is now hidden inside the model. Valley-fold the right portion of the flap to the left, with the crease beginning at the point at the top. Repeat behind.

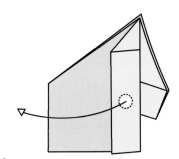

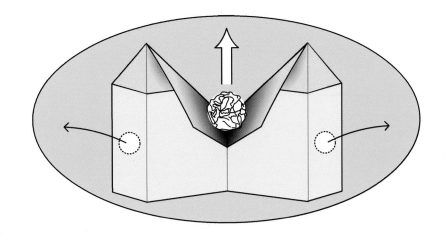

11 Holding the flap you made in step 10 at the circle, pull the model open.

The Catapult.
Place an object to launch, such as a crumpled ball of paper, into the trough. Hold the left and right flaps at the circles, and then pull the model apart quickly.

Football

This Football was popular back when I was in grade school, before I'd even heard the word "origami." It was this model that inspired me to write this book. I figured that anyone who likes to make the Football would enjoy making and playing lots of other games with paper.

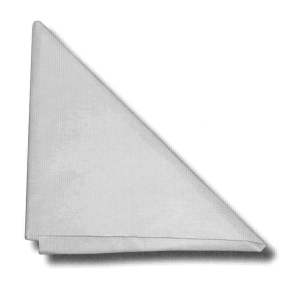

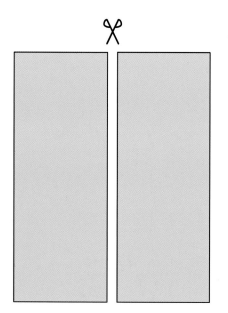

1 Cut the paper in half the long way. You can make two footballs—one from each piece.

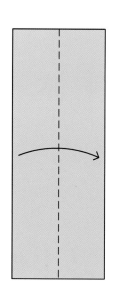

2 Fold the left edge to the right.

3 Fold the top edge to lie along the right edge.

4 Fold the model down along the base of the triangle.

5 Fold the top edge to lie along the left edge.

6 Fold the model down along the base of the triangle.

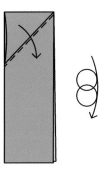

7 Fold the top edge to lie along the right edge. Then continue folding down and diagonally until the model looks like that shown in step 8.

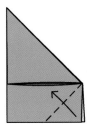

8 Fold the lower right corner of what's left of the paper to lie along the bottom of the upper triangle.

9 Tuck the remaining paper inside the pocket at the bottom of the triangle.

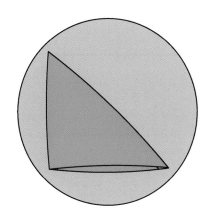

The Football.

Frog

I adapted this Frog from an index (3" x 5") card version that I learned many years ago. Because it can be made from any size rectangle, it's a great origami piece to make while waiting at a restaurant or a doctor's office.

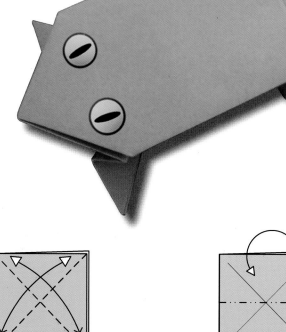

1 Fold the left edge to the right.

2 Fold and unfold the upper left and right corners to the opposite edges.

3 Mountain-fold and unfold the top edge down, so that the crease passes through the intersection of the creases made in step 2.

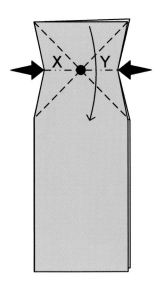

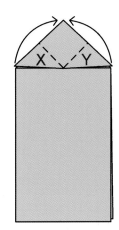

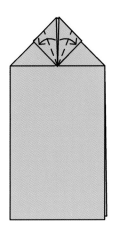

4 Press down the model at the dot, causing the shape to pop inside-out. Then, push in the sides while bringing down the top. Flaps X and Y will be created, and then hidden beneath the top flap.

5 Fold the left and right corners of the triangle to the top.

6 Fold the near layers of the triangular flaps outward to lie along the creases you made in step 5.

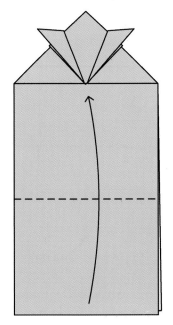

7 Fold the bottom edge up to the bottom of the large triangle.

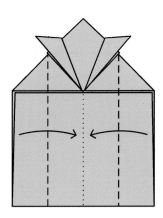

8 Fold the right and left edges to the center.

Frog | 35

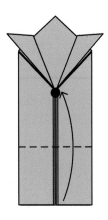

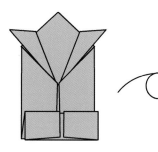

9 Fold the bottom edge up to the point indicated by the dot.

10 Fold down the flap created in step 9 to meet the bottom edge.

11 Turn the model over.

To make the frog hop or flip over, gently rub your finger down its back, applying slight pressure as you slide your finger off.

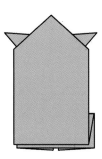

The Frog.

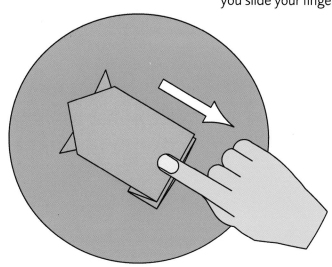

Triangle Chip

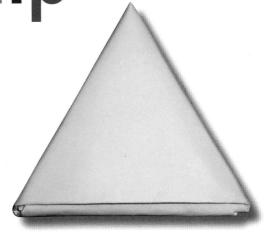

This is a sturdy model that can withstand lots of action—tossing, stacking, or sliding.

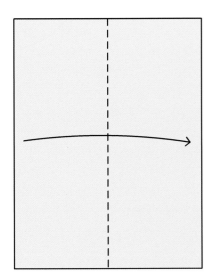

1 Fold the left edge to the right.

2 Fold the left edge to the right again.

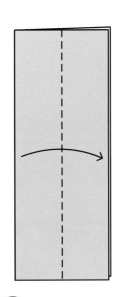

3 Fold the right edge to the left edge, then unfold. Do not crease all the way down.

4 Fold the top left corner so that it lies along the crease you made in step 3, shown with a dot.

  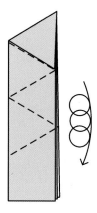

5 Fold the top right corner to lie along the left edge, creasing along the lower edge of the triangle you made in step 4.

6 Repeat step 5, this time folding to the right.

7 Repeat this maneuver three more times.

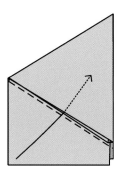

8 Tuck the remaining paper inside the pocket.

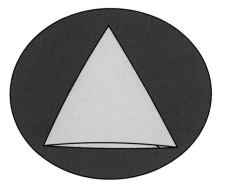

The Triangle Chip.

Pyramid

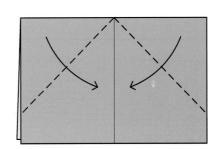

I like the fact that this model, with its triangular sides, appears impossible to have come from a flat sheet of rectangular paper, using no cuts or tape.

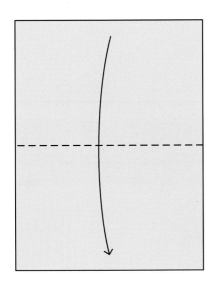

1 Fold the top edge to the bottom.

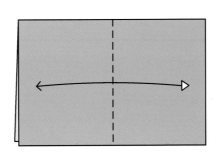

2 Fold and unfold the right edge to the left.

3 Fold the top left and right corners to the center crease.

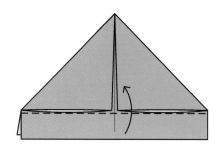

4 Fold up the near layer at the bottom to cover the flaps made in step 3.

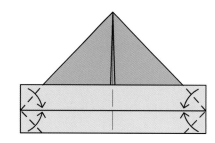

5 Fold the 4 corners inward as shown.

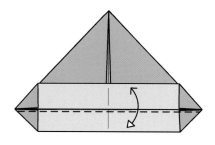

6 Fold and unfold the bottom flap as shown.

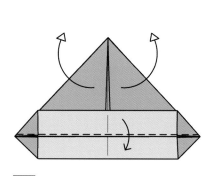

7 Fold the flap made in step 4 back down, and unfold the flaps made in step 3.

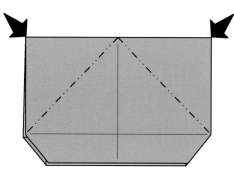

8 Push the left and right corners inside the model along existing creases.

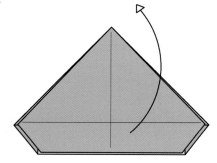

9 Lift up the top layer of the model so you can see inside.

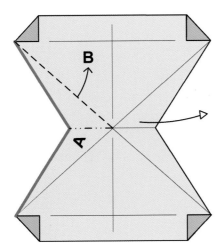

10 This is an underside view. Bring the edges shown in red together, then press flap A against panel B. Pull open the flap on the right.

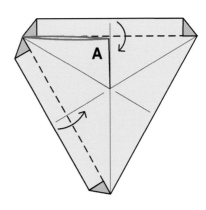

11 Note the position of the new flap. Fold the top hem inward to lock the new flap in place. Valley-fold the hem on the left inward.

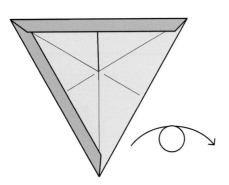

12 All folding is complete. Turn the model upside-down.

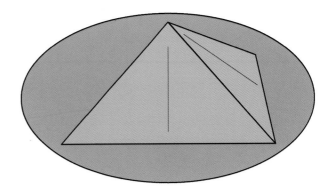

The Pyramid.

Goal Post

The Goal Post is made from two posts and one crossbar. There are many ways to configure the triangular flaps at the top of the Goal Post. I did it this way to balance the model so that it wouldn't tip over, as well as to create a trough in which to place the Crossbar. But this basic shape holds many possibilities that are fun to explore.

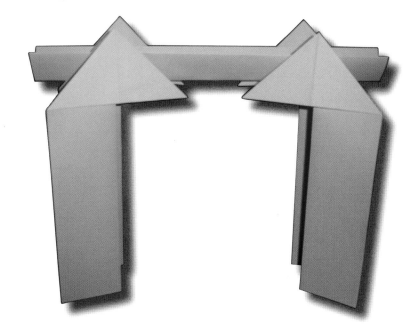

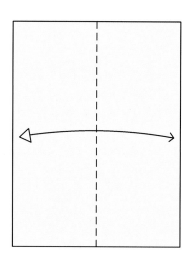

1 Fold and unfold the left edge to the right.

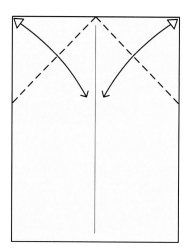

2 Fold and unfold the upper right and left corners to the center crease.

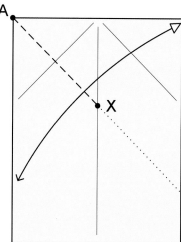

3 Bring the upper right corner down to the left edge, but only crease from A to X. Then unfold.

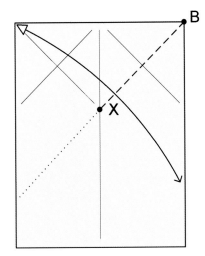

4 Bring the upper left corner down to the right edge, but only crease from B to X. Then unfold.

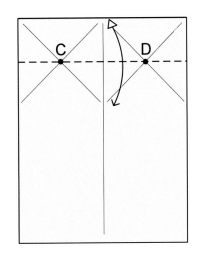

5 Make a crease that intersects C and D. Then unfold.

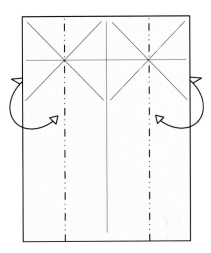

6 Mountain-fold and unfold the left edges to the center crease.

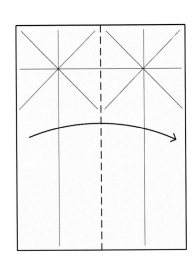

7 Fold the model in half along the center crease.

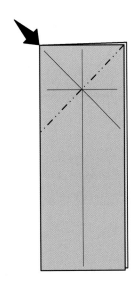

8 Push the upper left corner inside the model, using existing creases.

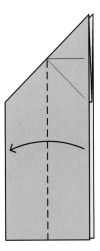

9 Swing the layer nearest you to the left along the existing crease. The top will open up.

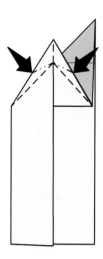

10 This is a 3-D view, looking inside a pyramid shape. Push in both sides of the pyramid along existing creases, pressing them flat against the model, and a new flap will appear, jutting out toward you.

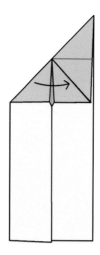

11 Swing this new flap to the right and lay it flat.

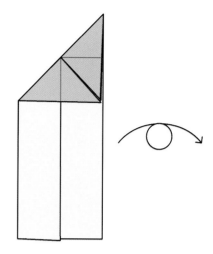

12 Turn the model over.

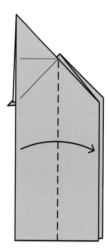

13 Swing the near layer to the right along the existing crease. The top will open up. This is the same as step 9, but on the other side.

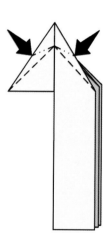

14 Again, push in the sides of the pyramid, and a new flap will appear, jutting out toward you.

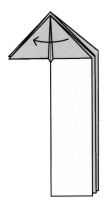

15 Swing this new flap to the left and lay it flat.

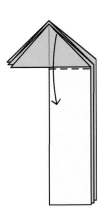

16 Fold the near layer of the triangular flap down.

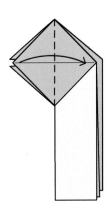

17 Fold the near layer all the way to the right.

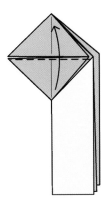

18 Return the flap you brought down in step 16 to its original position.

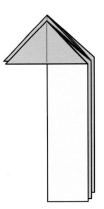

One post is complete. Make another one exactly the same.

Crossbar

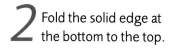

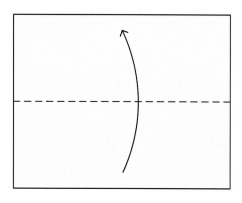

1 Fold the bottom edge to the top.

2 Fold the solid edge at the bottom to the top.

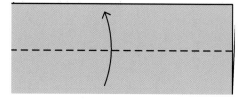

3 Last time, fold the solid edge at the bottom to the top.

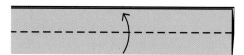

The Crossbar.

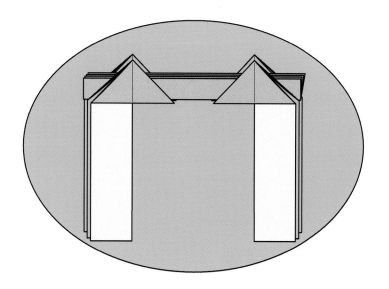

Straddle the crossbar between the two posts to complete your Goal Post.

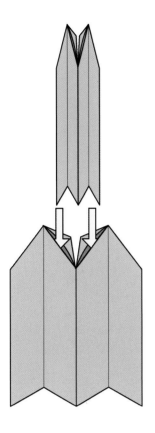

To double the height of the Goal Post, make two more post units. Then feed the two folded edges on the top piece into the two slots in the inner section of the bottom.

This is a view from the back.

Now straddle the crossbar between the two upper posts.

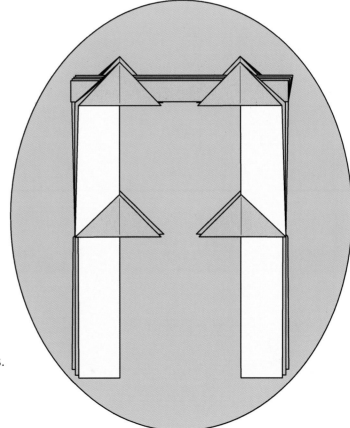

Crossbar | 47

Loop

The technique used to lock the loop is similar to one I learned when folding a ring out of a dollar bill. You could also make a chain by making one loop, then feeding one end of the next loop through it before connecting its ends, and repeating as necessary.

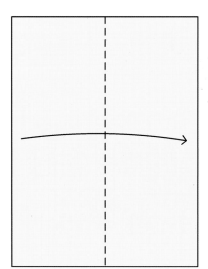

1 Fold the left edge to the right.

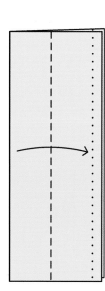

2 Fold the left edge to a little less than 1/2 inch from the right edge, indicated by the dotted line.

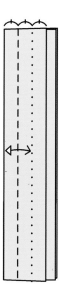

3 Fold the left edge to the dotted line, which should be about 1/3 the width of the near layer. Then unfold.

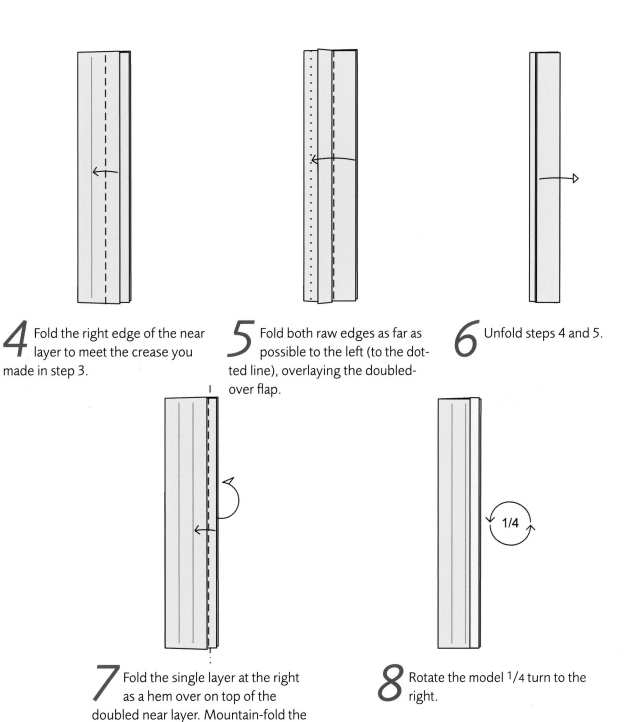

4 Fold the right edge of the near layer to meet the crease you made in step 3.

5 Fold both raw edges as far as possible to the left (to the dotted line), overlaying the doubled-over flap.

6 Unfold steps 4 and 5.

7 Fold the single layer at the right as a hem over on top of the doubled near layer. Mountain-fold the layer in back along the same edge.

8 Rotate the model 1/4 turn to the right.

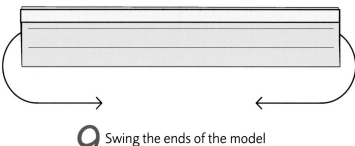

9 Swing the ends of the model together, feeding the right end into the left.

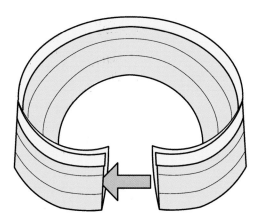

10 Push the right end into the left end about 3/4 of an inch.

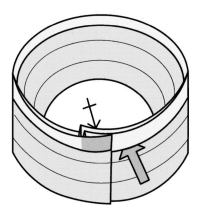

11 Lift up the hem on the right portion, shown by the arrow, and wrap it over over the left portion, covering the shaded area. Repeat this with the inside hem.

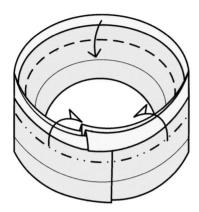

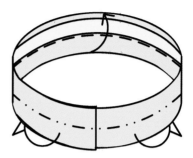

12 Fold the top third of the loop to the inside all the way around along the existing crease.

13 Fold the bottom portion of the loop to the inside all the way around along the existing crease, covering up the layer from step 12.

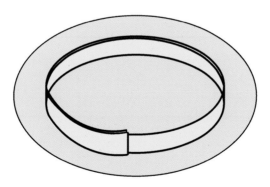

The Loop.

Saucer Ring

Not only can the Saucer Ring be thrown like a Frisbee® as in the "Flying Saucers" game (page 71), it can also serve as a target, like in "Glider Goal" (page 75). Either way, there are lots of fun possibilities with this model.

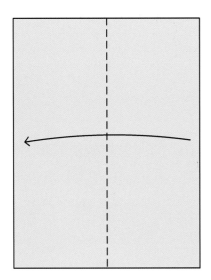

1 Fold the right edge to the left.

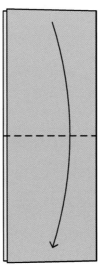

2 Fold the top edge to the bottom.

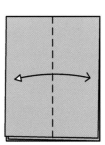

3 Fold and unfold the left edge to the right.

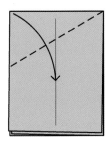

4 Fold the upper left corner to lie along the center crease.

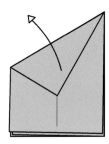

5 Unfold step 4.

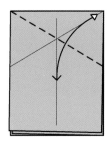

6 Repeat steps 4 and 5 on the upper right corner.

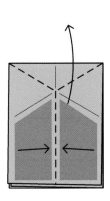

7 Pinch the darker areas of the top flap together, lifting the new flap up toward you.

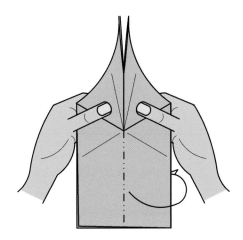

8 While the new flap is pointing up toward you, swing the right portion of the model around and behind.

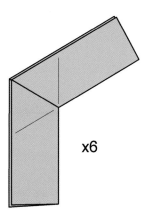

x6

9 This is the completed Saucer Ring unit. Make a total of 6.

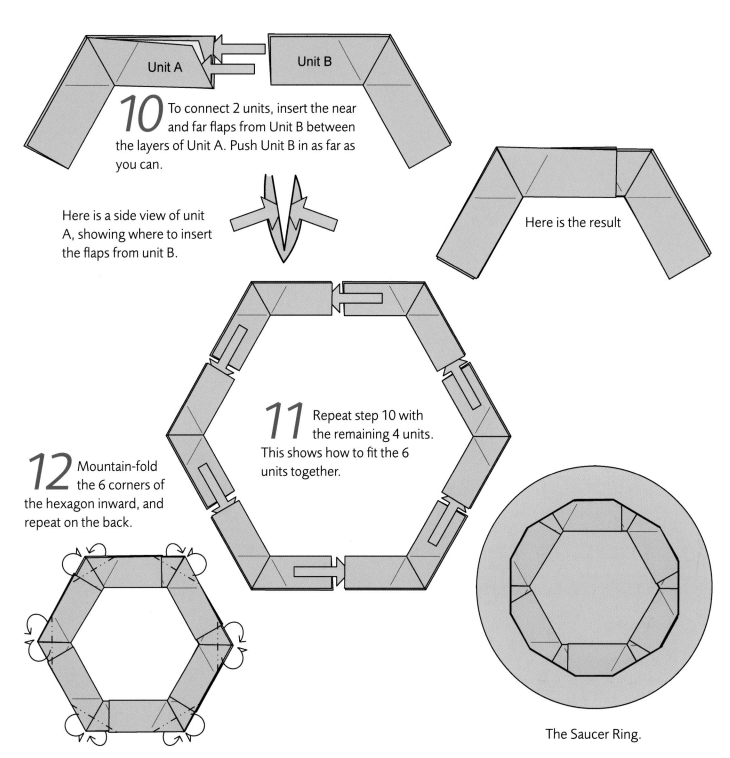

Unit A

Unit B

10 To connect 2 units, insert the near and far flaps from Unit B between the layers of Unit A. Push Unit B in as far as you can.

Here is a side view of unit A, showing where to insert the flaps from unit B.

Here is the result

11 Repeat step 10 with the remaining 4 units. This shows how to fit the 6 units together.

12 Mountain-fold the 6 corners of the hexagon inward, and repeat on the back.

The Saucer Ring.

Game Piece

There are many ways to decorate this Game Piece—in addition to drawing on it, you can glue on buttons or feathers, cover it with stickers, or even wrap pipe cleaners around it.

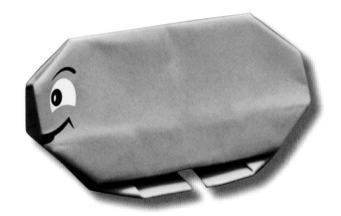

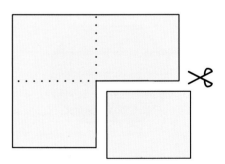

1 Fold a sheet of letter-size paper into fourths, then cut off one of the sections. You'll use this section of paper to make the Game Piece.

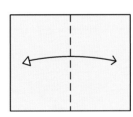

2 Fold and unfold the left edge to the right.

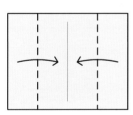

3 Fold both sides to the center.

Spinner

Besides writing numbers on the six spaces of this Spinner, you could use it as a fortune teller by writing different answers on the six spaces, asking it a question, and then spinning it. Or, you can color in the six spaces to make an optical toy.

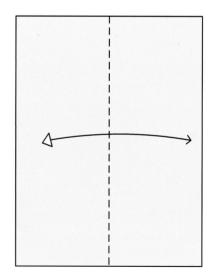

1 Fold the left edge to the right and unfold.

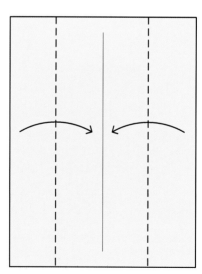

2 Fold the left and right edges to the center.

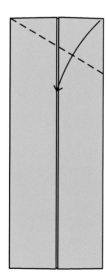

3 Beginning the crease at the top left corner, fold the top right corner to the center.

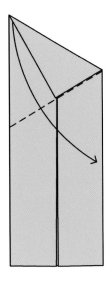

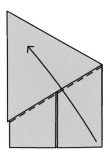

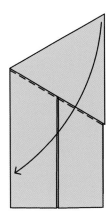

4 Fold the upper left corner down to lie along the right edge, creasing along the lower edge of the flap made in step 3.

5 Fold the upper right corner down to lie along the left edge, creasing along the lower edge of the triangle.

6 Fold the bottom portion of the model up along the lower edge of the triangle.

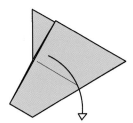

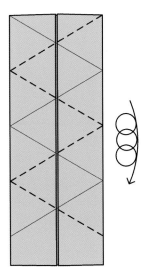

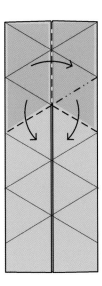

7 Unfold to step 3.

8 Repeat steps 3–7, this time beginning the crease at the top right corner, folding down the top left corner to the center. Then unfold to step 3.

9 Press the shaded areas together, creasing along the indicated fold lines. Then lay the resulting flap over to the right.

Spinner | 59

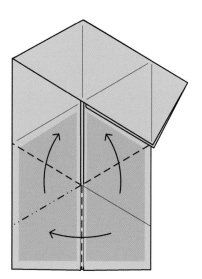

10 Repeat step 9 with the lower portion of the model, bringing the shaded areas together, and laying the resulting flap over to the left.

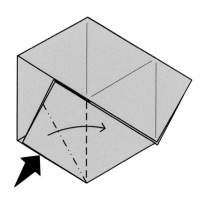

11 Lift and squash the lower flap along the indicated crease lines.

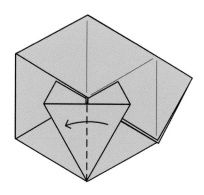

12 Fold the right side over to the left.

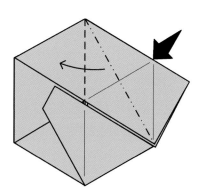

13 Lift and squash the upper flap along the indicated crease lines.

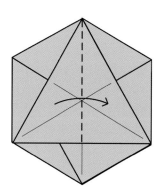

14 Fold the left side over to the right.

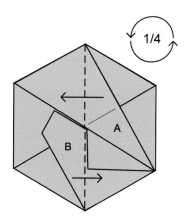

15 Lift doubled flaps A and B up so they stand up at 90 degrees from the plane of the model. Rotate the model 1/4 turn.

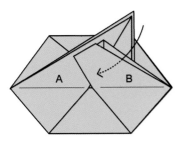 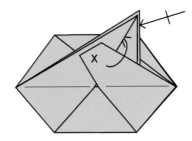 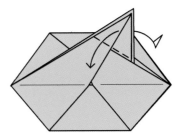

16 Here is a view showing the model in perspective. Lift doubled flap A and place it entirely between the two flaps of B.

17 Place flap X inside the pocket indicated. Repeat behind.

18 Fold the protruding triangular flaps down, one on each side.

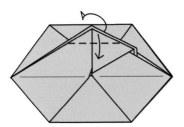 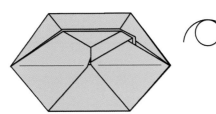

19 Fold the tip of the triangular flap downward to completely lock the handle. Repeat behind.

20 Here is the result. Turn the model over.

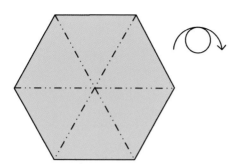

21 Reinforce all creases passing through the center with mountain folds. This makes the model spin better. Turn the model back over.

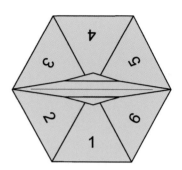

22 Number each of the six triangles to complete your spinner.

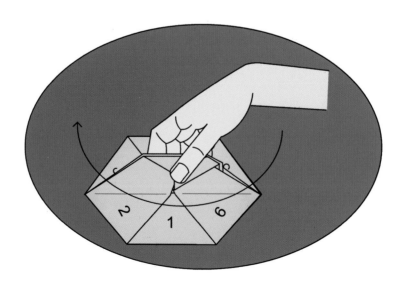

The Spinner.

Part II
The Games

Balancing Act

Object: Try to keep the Wing balanced on the Pyramid as long as possible while spinning it around.

Number of players: 2–4

Models needed: Wing (page 18)
Pyramid (page 39)

Setup: Balance the Wing on the tip of the Pyramid.

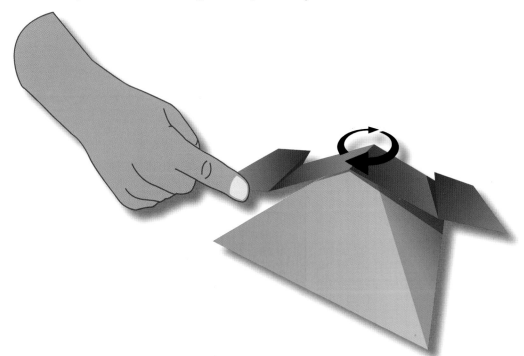

How to play:
1. Toss a coin to see who starts. Play proceeds clockwise.
2. Each player in turn taps the Wing to make it spin.
3. Play continues until the Wing falls off.
4. As a team, try adding more and more spins before the Wing falls off.

Basket Bombs

Object: Get the paper ball through the Hoop by hand or using the Catapult.

Number of players: 2–4

Models needed: Basketball Hoop (page 25)
Crumpled paper ball
Optional: Catapult (page 29)

Setup: Place the Basketball Hoop on a table.

How to play:
1. Players stand 3–5 feet from the Basketball Hoop.
2. Players take turns tossing the ball through the Hoop. Scoring is as follows:
   - By hand = 5 points
   - Using the Catapult = 10 points
3. The player with the highest score after 10 tosses is the winner.

Bowl 'Em Over

Object: Knock down the most Bowling Pins.

Number of players: 2–4

Models needed: 6 Bowling Pins (page 27)
Crumpled paper ball

Setup: Set up the Bowling Pins on the floor in rows of 1, 2, and 3.

How to play:
1. Each player gets only 1 throw per frame (unlike real bowling, where there are 2 throws per frame).
2. Players get 1 point for each pin knocked down, and an extra 5 points for a strike (all 6 pins).
3. Players take turns throwing and setting up pins.
4. The player with the highest score at the end of 10 frames is the winner.

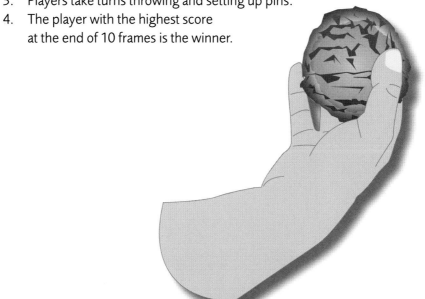

Bull's-Eye

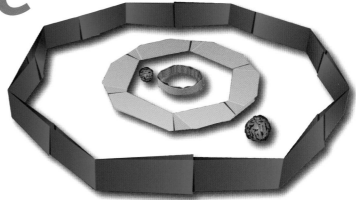

Object: Get the highest score by tossing the ball closest to the center of the target.

Number of players: 2–4

Models needed: Loop (page 48)
8 Zig-Zag Units (page 19)
Saucer Ring (page 52)
Crumpled paper ball

Setup: Set up the target on the floor or a table with three regions:
- Innermost region—Place the Loop on the floor.
- Middle region—Place the Saucer Ring around the Loop.
- Outermost region—Fold all 8 Zig-Zag Units in half, then open them slightly. Feed one end of each unit into the next, surrounding the Loop in an octagon shape.

How to play:
1. Players stand 3–5 feet from the target.
2. Players take turns tossing the ball at the target.
3. Scoring is as follows:
   - Inside the Loop = 100 points
   - Inside the Saucer Ring = 60 points
   - Inside the octagon = 30 points
4. The first player to reach 500 points is the winner.

Can You Top This?

Object: Build as high a tower of Chips as you can.

Number of players: 2

Models needed: 10 Triangle Chips (page 37)

Setup: The game can be played on a table or the floor.

How to play: Players take turns stacking Chips, one on top of the other, until the tower falls.

Chip Toss

Object: See how many chips you can juggle between two upside-down Pyramids.

Number of players: 1

Models needed: 2 Pyramids (page 39)
Up to 10 Triangle Chips (page 37)

Setup: Prepare the models.

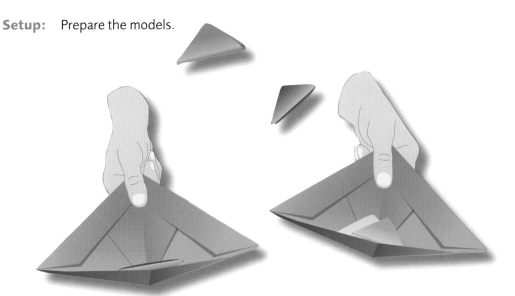

How to play:
1. Hold a Pyramid upside-down in each hand.
2. Place one Triangle Chip into a Pyramid, toss it into the air, and catch it with the other Pyramid.
3. Repeat going the other direction.
4. If you're successful with one Chip, add a second and try again.
5. Keep going until one or more Chips fall on the floor.

You can also play this game with more than one player. Each player holds a Pyramid, and tosses the Chip back and forth. With each successful round of catches, add a Chip. Keep going until someone misses.

Fill 'Er Up

Object: Get the most crumpled balls into the box.

Number of players: 2–4

Models needed: 1 Dragon per player (page 20)
Box (page 23)
Crumpled balls (20–30 per player, each player's a different color)

Setup: Place the box open side up in the center.

How to play:
1. Each player sits around the box with his/her Dragon's tail pointed toward the box.
2. Start a timer for one minute.
3. Players put a crumpled ball, one at a time, on the nose of their Dragons, and tap the center section. This launches the ball backwards, and hopefully, into the box.
4. After one minute, players count how many balls they got in the box.
5. The player who gets the most balls into the box is the winner.

Flying Saucers

Object: Throw and catch the Saucer Ring.

Number of players: 2 or more

Models needed: Saucer Ring (page 52)

Setup: Players spread out in a circle.

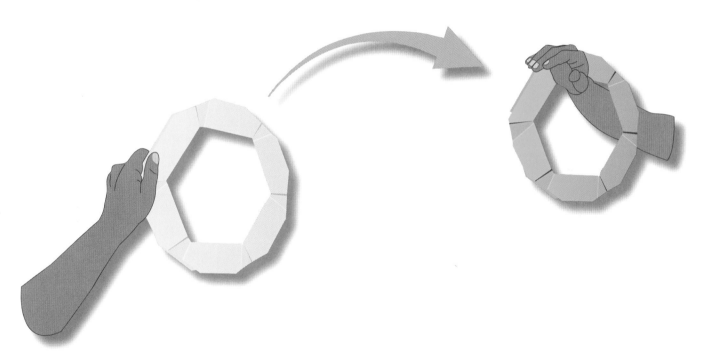

How to play: Players toss the Saucer Ring around, trying to catch it without using their hands, just by holding up an arm.

Football

Object: Score the most points with touchdowns and field goals.

Number of players: 2–4

Models needed: Football (page 32)
2 sets of Goal Posts (page 42)

Setup: Set up the Goal Post.

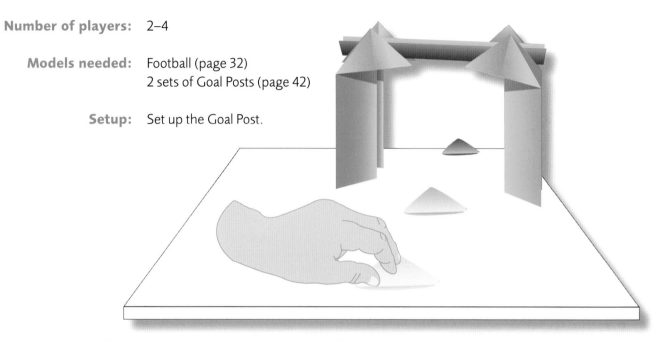

How to play:
1. Players sit on opposite sides of a table.
2. Toss a coin to see who starts.
3. Player 1 slides the Football to the opposite side under the Goal Post, trying to get it to stop with part of it sticking over the edge of the table. That's a touchdown. If it doesn't reach the edge, or goes over, there are no points, and it's Player 2's turn.
4. The player who makes a touchdown gets to try for an extra point. This is done by flicking the Football over the Goal Post. See page 85 for a picture of how to hold the Football for flicking.
5. Scoring is as follows:
   - Touchdown = 6 points
   - Football over bar = 2 points.
   - Football over double-high bar = 4 points.
     Page 28 describes how to set up a double-high goal post.
6. The first player to get 21 points is the winner.

Froggie Olympics

Object: Get the most points by making the Frog jump into, over, or onto the Box.

Number of players: 2–4

Models needed: Frog — 1 per player (page 34)
Box (page 23)

Setup: Place the Box on the table, and give each player a Frog.

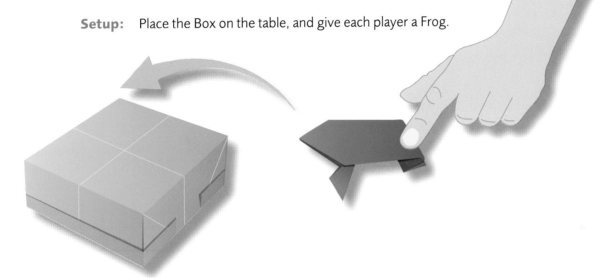

How to play:

1. Toss a coin to see who goes first, then proceed clockwise.
2. Each player on their turn gets to decide their level of difficulty—the more difficult, the more points:
   - If the Box is set open side facing up, getting the Frog to jump into the box = 5 points.
   - If the Box is set open side facing down or up, getting the Frog to jump over the box = 10 points.
   - If the Box is set open side facing down, getting the Frog to land on top of the box = 15 points.
   - If the player doesn't succeed in achieving their goal = 0 points.
3. After 5 rounds, the player with the highest score is the winner.

Ghost Dodgers

Object: Slide the Triangle Chip under the Ghost so that it doesn't fall over.

Number of players: 2–4

Models needed: Ghost (page 8)
Triangle Chip (page 37)

Setup: Stand the Ghost up at one end of a table.

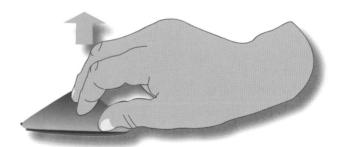

How to play: 1. Slide the Chip at the Ghost so that it passes underneath it. Scoring is as follows:
- The Ghost does not fall over = 1 point
- The Ghost falls over = 0 points
2. Play passes to the next player.
3. The player with the most points after 5 rounds is the winner.

Glider Goal

Object: Toss the Glider through the Saucer Ring from farther and farther away.

Number of players: 2

Models needed: Glider (page 10)
Saucer Wing (page 52)

Setup: Players stand a few feet apart, with Player 1 holding the Saucer Ring, and Player 2 holding the Glider.

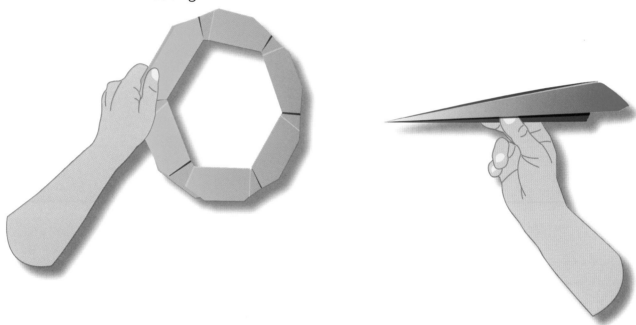

How to play:
1. Player 2 tries to toss the Glider through the Saucer Ring. Player 1 can move the Ring around to help.
2. If it goes through, each player takes a step back, and Player 2 tosses again.
3. With each successful toss, players take one more step back.
4. When Player 2 misses, they switch roles, with players standing a few feet apart again.

Leap Frog

Object: Keep the game going as long as possible.

Number of players: 1 or 2

Models needed: 2 Frogs (page 34)

Setup: Set one Frog behind the other.

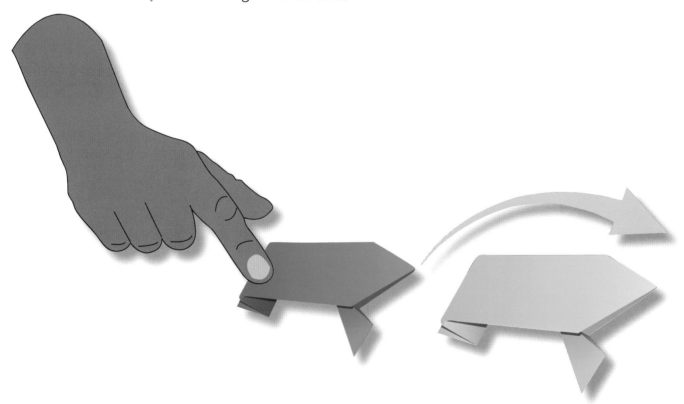

How to play:
1. Players take turns leaping their Frog over the other player's.
2. The round ends when a player fails to get his or her Frog to hop over the other's.

Non-Bored Game

Object: Create a board game, and be the first player to get from the beginning of the board to the end.

Number of players: 2–4

Models needed: Spinner (page 58)
2 or more Game Pieces (page 55)
1 or more Game Board units (page 12)
Triangle Chip (page 37)

Setup:
1. Make a Game Piece for each player, each decorating his or her own.
2. Color one corner of the Triangle Chip.
3. Decide how many spaces you want on your Game Board. Then make enough Game Board units to give you that many spaces. Each unit can have up to 16 spaces, but you can have spaces be two or three spaces wide. The example on the following page shows two Game Boards taped together.
4. Decide on a theme for the game, like movies, TV shows, music, or books, and invent funny things to do when landing on a space that relate to the theme. Or don't use a theme at all; just make up silly things to do, like in the example.
5. Decide on a name for the game.

How to play:
1. The youngest player gets to start. Play proceeds clockwise.
2. Spin the Spinner, and when it stops, the number closest to the colored point of the Triangle Chip determines the number of spaces the player moves.
3. Do whatever it says on the space.
4. The first person to the end is the winner.

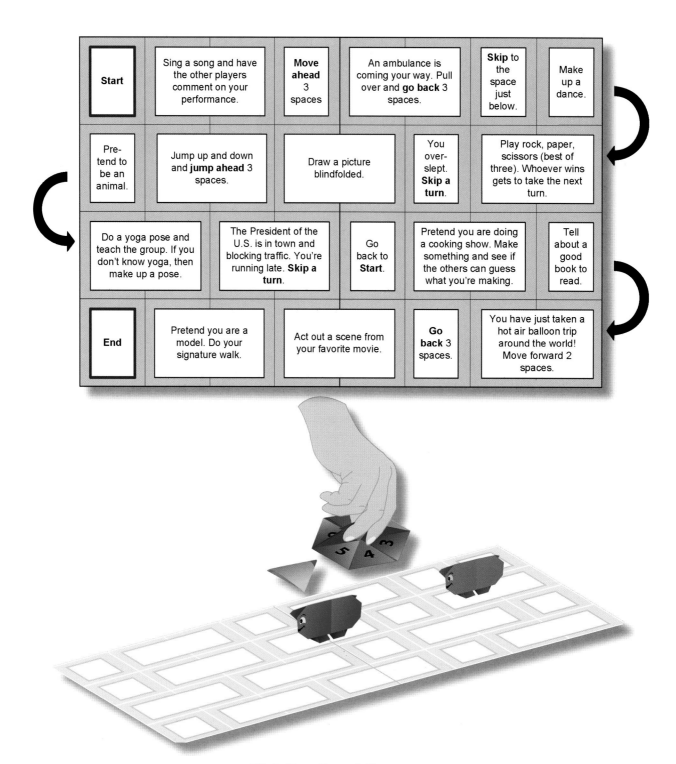

Start	Sing a song and have the other players comment on your performance.	**Move ahead 3 spaces**	An ambulance is coming your way. Pull over and **go back** 3 spaces.	**Skip** to the space just below.	Make up a dance.
Pretend to be an animal.	Jump up and down and **jump ahead** 3 spaces.	Draw a picture blindfolded.	You overslept. **Skip a turn**.	Play rock, paper, scissors (best of three). Whoever wins gets to take the next turn.
Do a yoga pose and teach the group. If you don't know yoga, then make up a pose.	The President of the U.S. is in town and blocking traffic. You're running late. **Skip a turn**.	Go back to **Start**.	Pretend you are doing a cooking show. Make something and see if the others can guess what you're making.	Tell about a good book to read.
End	Pretend you are a model. Do your signature walk.	Act out a scene from your favorite movie.	**Go back** 3 spaces.	You have just taken a hot air balloon trip around the world! Move forward 2 spaces.

Pick-Up Chips

Object: Win the most Chips.

Number of players: 2–4

Models needed: 10 Triangle Chips (page 37)
4 Zig-Zag Units (page 14)

Setup: 1. Fold all 4 Zig-Zag Units in half, then open them half way.
2. Feed one end of each Zig-Zag Unit into the next, until you have a square.
3. Pull the Zig-Zag Units apart a bit until each side is about 12 inches long.

How to play: 1. Toss a coin to see who goes first.
2. Drop all 10 Chips into the square.
3. Try to remove the Chips one at a time without disturbing (moving slightly) any other Chips.
4. If you disturb another Chip, it's the other player's turn.
5. When there are no more Chips, the player with the most Chips is the winner.

P'tui

Object: Win all the other player's Loops.

Number of players: 2

Models needed: 20 Loops (page 48)

Setup: Make 10 Loops using one color of paper, and 10 of another color. Or put some mark on one set of 10 to distinguish them from the other set.

How to play:

1. Players sit on opposite sides of a table, 10 Loops for each.
2. Player 1 flicks his Loop at Player 2's Loop, trying to knock it off the table without his own Loop falling off. If successful, he or she keeps the opponent's Loop.
3. If both Loops fall off, or if no contact is made, no Loops are claimed and gameplay passes to player 2.
4. The one who clears all of the other player's Loops is the winner.

Relay Rings

Object: Be the first team to complete the race.

Number of players: At least 8 (2 teams, 4 per team)

Models needed: 1 Zig-Zag Unit per player (page 14)
1 Loop per team (page 48)

Setup: 1. Half of each team lines up facing the other half, about 30 yards apart.
2. Give each player a Zig-Zag Unit, which is held with the single trough side up.
3. The person at the head of each line on one side places a Loop in his/ her trough.

How to play:

1. At the whistle, the players with the Loops walk/run as quickly as possible across the field, without letting the Loop fall out.
2. When reaching the other side, they pass the Loop to the first person in line by sliding it from trough to trough.
3. That player then moves to the back of the line, and the person now holding the Loop crosses the field to give it to the person at the head of the line on the opposite side, then moves to the back of the line.
4. Play continues until all players are in their original places.
5. The first team in its original place is the winner.

If the Loop falls to the ground at any point during the crossing, the player who dropped it must return to his or her starting line.

Ring Toss

Object: Get the most points by throwing the Loop over the Tube.

Number of players: 2–4

Models needed: 5 Loops (page 48)
Tube (page 15)
Coffee mug
Scrap paper

Setup:
1. Place the Tube in a coffee mug, and stuff scrap paper around it so that it fits snugly and stands upright.
2. Place the mug with the Tube on the floor.

How to play:
1. Stand 3–5 feet from the Tube.
2. Players take turns tossing the 5 Loops, one at a time, trying to get them over the Tube.
3. A player gets 10 points for each successful toss.
4. After tossing all 5 Loops, it's the next player's turn.
5. The player with the most points after 3 rounds is the winner.

Slay the Dragon

Object: Score the most points by knocking the Dragon off the Goal Post with the Football.

Number of players: 2–4

Models needed: Dragon (page 20)
Goal Post (page 42)
Football (page 32)

Setup:
1. Set up the Goal Post.
2. Hang the Dragon over the crossbar as shown.

How to play:
1. Flip a coin to see who goes first.
2. Flick the Football at the Dragon.
3. Scoring is as follows:
   - Knock the Dragon down without knocking down the Goal Post = 10 points.
   - Knock the Dragon down along with the Goal Post = 5 points.
   - Knock nothing down = 0 points.
4. Play passes to the next player.
5. After 10 turns per player, the one with the highest score is the winner.

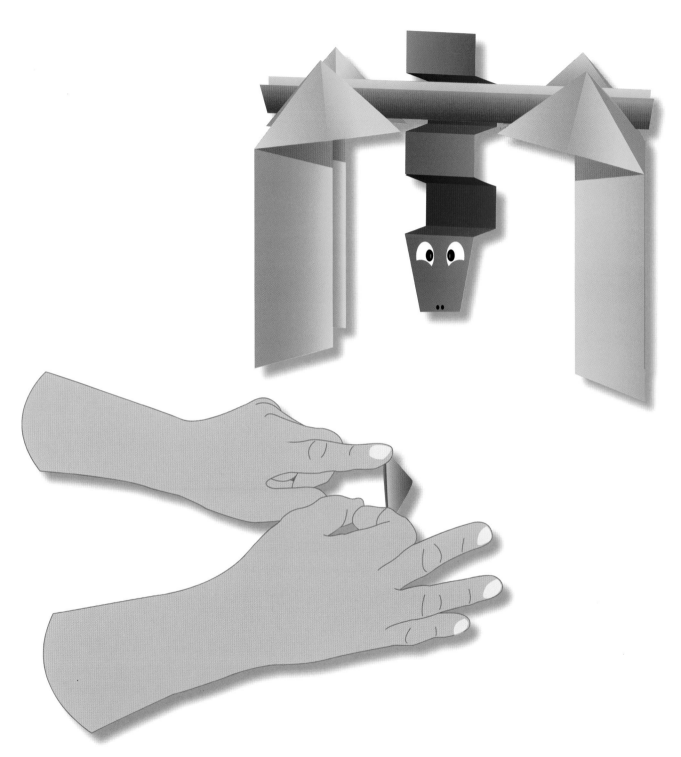

Snap Dragon

Object: Get the most pennies past the Dragon.

Number of players: 2

Models needed: Dragon (page 20)
Pennies (10)

Setup: Players sit across the table from each other.
Player 1 has the 10 pennies, and Player 2 controls the Dragon.

How to play:

1. Player 1 slides a penny across the table, trying to get it under and past the Dragon. Player 2 tries to stop the penny by pressing down on the middle of the Dragon's back.
2. If Player 1 gets the penny past the Dragon, Player 1 gets a point. If Player 2 stops the penny, Player 2 gets a point.
3. After the 10 pennies have been played, the players switch roles.
4. The person with the most points after each has played 5 rounds is the winner.

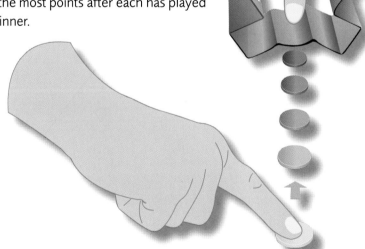

Stormy Seas

Object: Get the Sailboat from one end of the path to the other in the shortest time.

Number of players: 2–4

Models needed: Sailboat (page 16)
10 or more Zig-Zag Units (page 14)

Setup:
1. Fold each Zig-Zag Unit in half, then unfold it.
2. Connect 5 Zig-Zag Units together by feeding one Unit into the next to make a crooked wall. Make a second wall parallel to the first.

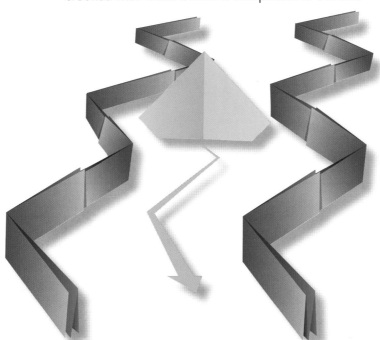

How to play:
1. Players take turns blowing the Sailboat through the crooked path, one blow per player.
2. Time how long it takes to get the Sailboat from one end to the other.
3. As a team, try to improve your time through the path.

Using Origami in the Curriculum

Here are some suggestions on how origami might be used across the curriculum:

Mathematics

Origami helps make abstract geometric forms tangible. For instance, you can demonstrate by folding paper how squares are composed of triangles, or how a 90-degree angle is made from two 45-degree angles. In fact, the Israeli Origami Center has created an entire curriculum that uses origami to teach geometry to children in elementary schools. For more information, do an Internet search for "origametria" and "origami and math."

Science

- Paper can be pleated, compressed, and released to demonstrate the principle of potential and kinetic energy.
- Paper airplanes can be used to demonstrate principles of aerodynamics.
- Origami, which relies considerably on right/left symmetry, can serve as a jumping off point for a discussion of symmetry found within nature.
- Origami has been shown to have scientific applications, such as for collapsing large objects that later on need to be expanded. Examples include car air bags, space telescope lenses, or stents to open up arteries and veins. You can ask students to see if they can think of any other examples. For more information, do an Internet search for "airbag folding."

Art

- There are many origami models, such as cubes, spheres, and chains, that are made from many simple units or modules joined together, usually without glue or tape. For a fun activity, have all the students fold the units, and then ask someone to connect them and mount the finished work for display. These kinds of projects bring participants together toward a common goal. For more information, do an Internet search for "modular origami."
- Origami can be either highly realistic or abstract. For example, paperfolders have created extremely detailed elephants possessing every feature—tusks, ears, four legs, and tail. They've also created elephants with a mere suggestion of a trunk, or simple pleats for ears. An interesting question to discuss with students is "What are the differences between realistic and abstract art?"

Special Needs

Children with special needs who have learned a few origami models are given a sense of accomplishment, and a way to shine in front of all of their peers.

Developmental Benefits of Origami

Origami can stimulate development in many ways:

Independence from Technology

Although computers and other types of digital technology have obvious benefits, they also make it easy for us to become passive consumers, rather than actively engaged. Origami can help restore our ability to engage in and make discoveries about the physical world, using our hands and imagination. An added benefit—paper is inexpensive and recyclable.

Brain Development

Doing origami stimulates both the left (logical) and right (creative) hemispheres of our brains, whether we reproduce others' designs or create our own. Research has shown that the tactile, motor, and visual zones in our brains are engaged and active when we do origami.

Life Skills

Origami teaches patience, analytical skills, and delayed gratification, all of which are valuable qualities that can help us to be successful in life.

Share Your Ideas

I'd love to hear about how you are using Origami Games—and origami in general—in your classroom. Please drop me a line via the "Contact Me" link on my website www.joeldstern.com.

Additional Resources

Books
There are hundreds of origami books available in many different languages. Here are a few in English geared toward beginning folders:

- *Origami Birthday Party* by Florence Temko, Tuttle Publishing

- *Origami Spectacular!* by Michael LaFosse, Tuttle Publishing

- *Minigami: Mini Origami Projects for Cards, Gifts and Decorations* by Gay Merrill Gross, Firefly Books

Paper
You can find origami paper at most art supply stores. Here are two sources on the web:

- *Kim's Crane* – www.kimscrane.com

- *The Paper Tree* – www.paper-tree.com

These sources also carry origami books.

Online Communities
There are several listservs for origami, and this is the oldest one, going back to 1988. It also has searchable archives.

- *origami-L Listserv* – lists.digitalorigami.com/mailman/listinfo/origami

Web Sites

You can find just about anything you want to know about origami on the Internet. Here are some of the most popular and useful sites:

- *Origami Swami* – swami.giladorigami.com
  A set of links to models from around the world. Excellent for beginners.

- *Origami Database* – www.origamidatabase.com
  A comprehensive directory of origami models, searchable by model, designer, and book title.

- *Gilad Aharoni's Web Site* – www.giladorigami.com
  Reviews of many new origami books and journals.

- *Origami Resource Center* – www.origami-resource-center.com
  Links to diagrams, databases, book reviews; describes ways to be a part of the paperfolding community.

- *Web Site of Robert J. Lang* – www.langorigami.com
  Stunningly beautiful and complex models, and lots of information about the scientific applications of origami.

Organizations

Below are the two largest origami organizations in the English-speaking world. On their web sites you'll find lots of information, including listings of local area groups.

- *Origami-USA* – www.origami-usa.org

- *British Origami Society* – www.britishorigami.info

Acknowledgments

This book is dedicated to my wife Susan for making it all possible, and to my children Rena, Ethan, and Anna for all the fun and games.

I'm very grateful to the following people for their contributions to this book:

- Konstantin Vints, for the beautiful images that grace the Games section of the book

- My nephew Harry Chiel, for diligently proofreading the folding instructions

- Vivian Levy and her third grade class, for showing me a world of game possibilities

- Jim Grande, for suggesting the idea for the book

- Florence Temko, for her warm friendship over the years, and for her keen suggestions

- Shelley Lawrence, for her enthusiastic support

- Michael LaFosse, for his encouragement

- Robert Sabuda, for his amazing talent and generous spirit

- Ariel Albornoz, Peter Chen, Alex Willis Garcini, Lisa Kaplan, Leslie Lawson, Paul Lupi and Brad Saunders for their useful suggestions

- My daughter Anna, for her terrific game board ideas

- Norman and Lela Jacoby, and Petty and Bates Metson for their ongoing love and support

About the Author

Hallie Lerman

Joel Stern has enjoyed origami since his childhood. A native of Omaha, Nebraska, he has conducted many origami workshops for all ages in camps, schools, community centers, and libraries. Joel is also the author of *Animated Origami Faces*, *Jewish Holiday Origami*, as well as *Washington Pops!*, a collection of do-it-yourself pop-up cards of famous buildings in Washington, D.C. His origami and pop-up creations have been exhibited in the U.S., Japan, and Israel. Joel lives in Los Angeles with his wife Susan and their three children. He can be reached via his website www.joeldstern.com.

My Origami Games

Name of the game: _____

Object of the game: _____

Models needed for the game, and number of each:

Model	Number

Number of players: _____

Rules of the game:

_____

_____

_____

_____

_____

_____

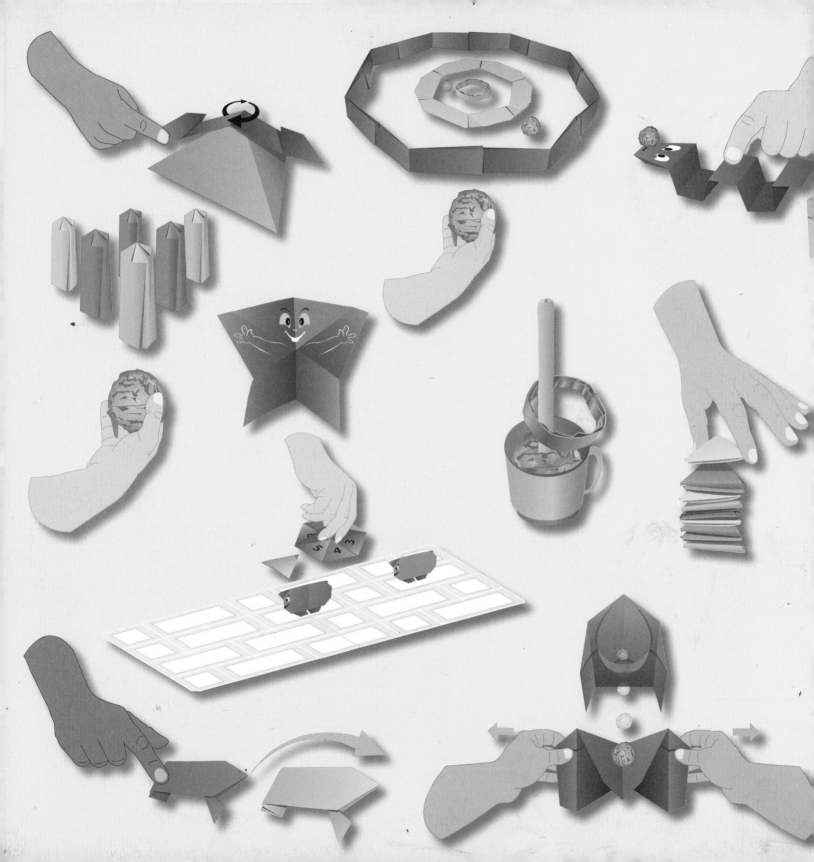